THE LAST
WITCH
TRIAL

D1824756

THE LAST WITCH TRIAL

SIDDHARTH NIRWAN

Notion Press

Old No. 38, New No. 6
McNichols Road, Chetpet
Chennai - 600 031

First Published by Notion Press 2016
Copyright © Siddharth Nirwan 2016
All Rights Reserved.

ISBN 978-93-86009-29-6

DEDICATION PAGE

To all women who have suffered from false accusations of Witchcraft

AUTHOR'S NOTE

All characters, places, and events in this novel are fictitious. Any resemblance or similarity to any of them is purely coincidental and unintentional. Factual narratives have been liberally interspersed with the fiction to provide ambience and complexion to the plot. In order not to distract the reader from the main theme, references to the facts have been deliberately deducted. Anyone interested in them can simply refer to online resources or author's social networking sites. Objective of this novel is to entertain and not to endorse anything supernatural.

Acknowledgements

'*Behind every successful man is a woman,*' somebody said. '*Behind every successfully written book is also a woman,*' he missed out.

This book would not have been successfully written if not for the unalterable backing and ever enduring conviction in me by my wife, Mahima. And this page is futile if it does not speak emphatically about her. If writing a novel someday was my dream, transforming it into actuality was her vision.

My parents, Shri Prem Singh and Smt Suchitra, who have always have supported and emboldened me in all aspects of life, selflessly.

My son, Aaryav, whose mere presence has deluded my life with beatitude and ecstasy.

My colleagues at workplace; Shubham, Dhara and Mahesh, who were the first readers and first appraisers of my work.

My college buddy, Sunay Bhatt, for creating wonderful music for my story. *Hail Redemption Creed!*

My cousin, Jaya, for her valuable input for the cover design concept.

To entire Notion Press Team, without whom, our dream and vision would have still been a dream, a vision, and not an actual book.

A BRIEF HISTORY OF WITCH TRIALS

The World

If the early modern period (1400–1800 AD) was considered as a significant era in terms of globalization, exploration and colonization of new lands, and radicalization of world trade, it cannot be forgotten for the lamentable incidents of witch trials that took place on a massive scale, especially on the European land and other parts of the world. During this period, hundreds of thousands of women were falsely tried for witchcraft and executed; majority of them were carried out under the orders of the Church.

Most of them were burned alive, some were pelted to death, and some were hanged publicly. In fact, a slang any woman feared the most that time was '*a witch.*'

Height of the mass hysteria can be calculated from the fact that in 1487, an entire treatise was published in Germany, by Heinrich Kramer (a Catholic clergyman) on the persecution of witches, *Malleus Maleficarum*. It describes in detail how to identify and convict witches, various tests that can prove that they really are witches, claim that those who practiced witchcraft were more often women, systematically refute arguments claiming that witchcraft does not exist. *The book was a best seller of the era, only next to the Bible, and it still survives in the modern times.*

Among the most infamous were: the *Trier* witch trials (1581–93), the *Fulda* witch trials (1603–06), the *Wurzburg* witch trials (1626–1631), the *Bamberg* witch trials (1626–31) and the *Salem* witch trials (1692–93).

In Great Britain, the Witchcraft Act passed in 1735, officially marked their end. However, sporadic witch trials continued through the second half of the eighteenth century, which too later declined in number and later were rarely heard of.

In the twentieth century, *Wicca* was founded in England. Also known as *Pagan Witchcraft*, it was a religious movement that was started by a small group of dedicated followers who hypothesized that those prosecuted and killed in the name of witchcraft were not followers of Satan (as they were accused of), but mere followers of a pre-Christian pagan religion. It celebrates woman as a goddess and is practiced in many parts of the world successfully as a full-formed religion.

India

As far as the Indian context of witch trials or witch-hunting is considered, it is unclear when it exactly emerged on the scene. However, unlike the western world, where 'witch-hunting' is now in the history books or documentary videos, the situation in India is still very grim.

It can be realized from the fact that between 1991 and 2010, according to the National Crimes Bureau, more than 1,700 women were murdered in the name of witchcraft.

In one of the most recent data, *117 were killed in a year alone.*

In 2001, the Jharkhand government even passed the *'Daayan Pratha'* or the *'Prevention of witch practices'* to stop the increasing atrocities against women. But after more than a decade, witch-hunting is still rampant in the state, where more than hysteria it has become a disturbing trend.

A year ago, I happened to watch a documentary on *'Indian witch-hunt.'* I stood aghast to know how a teenage boy in Jharkhand killed his aunt merely of suspicion that she was a witch and responsible for the death of his father and elder brother. What was more horrific about the incident was that the boy single handedly cut off her head with just a razor blade. He later walked with the chopped head in the entire village, poised to local news channels and conceded boldly to the police. Later, on being interviewed by a journalist he did not show any signs of remorse for what he had done. According to him, he did it because a local witch doctor conjectured his aunt to be a witch and the boy did not want to die at her hands, like his father and brother.

The boy was not just a criminal. He was also a part of that disturbing trend.

PROLOGUE

My name is Ajay, just Ajay. Well, born on the holy land, known to rest of the world as the land of ethos, spirituality and 'Great Indian' values, I too used to have a surname once. My complete name was Ajay Singh Thakur since my birth until five years ago, when a turn of events made me drop the latter; the reason for doing so shall become obvious later to the reader.

It was a week before Diwali, during the 'festive ablution' of our house; a de rigueur custom in every Hindu family, that I discovered my old brass trunk in the storehouse. In the past five years, I had utterly forgotten about it. I took it out to the living room. It had such a firm layer of dust stuck like a magnet to it that it took me almost half an hour to wipe it off and make its metallic silver body finally apparent. There was small lock riveted to its latch. *'Where could I possibly find its key?'* It seemed a very wacky question that I eventually did not ask myself. As the lock wasn't too rebellious, two strikes of a mallet were decent enough to crack it down.

I opened it and glanced inside. My hand written diary was neatly stacked along with few other documents in the same manner as I had stowed them in it five years ago.

I took out my diary and started to read it randomly. As I did so, the trauma of those dark and uneventful times during which it was written came alive in my psyche. I had vowed to myself that I shall never open the trunk. But today on seeing it after ages, I just could not control myself.

When five years ago the nefarious incident took place at Jaisinghpur, there were lots of rumors fecundated by the local people and the media. Everyone construed the facts to their own fantasies. But as someone who was one of the most integral part of the events, I knew that all of them were far from actuality.

However, that chapter was shut down in everyone's reminiscence long ago. Nobody cared to commemorate it except for a few victims, that included me.

That entire night I spent twisting and twirling in my bed.

All that had been briefed about the 'Jaisinghpur Witch Murders' was nothing but shear baloney!

I myself was clocked up in recovering from the shock, that I do not recollect accurately what statement I had given to the police and media at that time.

The truth needs to be told! It damn needs to be told by people who witnessed it to the core!

But, my diary notes of those times were not sufficient; they would just produce half of the story. I needed the other half from Professor Shashank Arya. I called him up the next morning. We both were strangers earlier, though he was a professor in the same university of which I was a student that time. Since then we became good friends. I asked him if he could narrate his version of the story in some kind of format. But, he aghasted me by declaring that he had recorded his own narration of the events in audio tapes, as they happened and had not discarded them till now.

He was astir enough despite his busy schedule to arrange and dispatch them to me within a week.

However, still there are deficits in the story that could not be fulfilled by my diary and Professor's tapes alone. Hence, I have added to the best of my memory, few narrations to supplement it.

The following pages that you are going to turn is a collection of diary notes, audio recordings, newspaper excerpts, narrations and other formats; all arranged in a chronological order. Some people call it an *epistolary.*

The following pages that you are going to turn is a collection of ethos burned, spirituality denuded and 'Great Indian' values gang raped in broad daylight. And all that happened on the same holy land on which I, and probably you were born too.

I, Ajay, am going to narrate to you a true epistolary as it happened. It is the story of Maya; a woman, a daughter, a mother, a wife, and what the people of this same holy land turned her into; an evil, a mass murderer, a beast and a... WITCH!

Ajay
November 24, 2015

CHAPTER 1

THE CALL

Ajay's Diary
October 25, 2010–11 pm

I had been sleeping the whole afternoon when my phone buzzed. It was perhaps ringing since several minutes; but my terrible sleep deluded me as if it was some music playing outside.

Soon, I realized that it was the same ringtone I had transcribed from Anjana's cell phone a few months ago. Anjana was jaded of my previous ringtone, which had loitered on my phone for the past one year. With bankrupt eyes, I stirred my hands in search of it. I usually used to keep it on a small table just beside my bed. Instead, my hand touched something else.

Before I could realize, I heard the sound of shattering of glass. I opened my eyes and browsed around. I saw pieces of glass with milk splashed all over the floor. Rahim had started to keep a tumbler of milk every night at my bedside, so that if I wake up in the midst of night; instead searching for liquor, I could satisfy my quench with something hearty.

He was righteous in doing so. During the past three weeks, I consumed more alcohol than I did in my entire lifetime.

Perhaps no reason is good enough to become an inveterate alcoholic, but I had one.

Anjana was getting married to someone else, and that too by her assent. Her father never envisioned his daughter's future nowhere near to propitious with a guy whose own parentage was devastated and who was pursuing studies in Arts something which was meant for those who qualified just enough to be a wastrel, at least in this rickety country.

She had been engaged to some bloody investment banker settled in Canada, who also happened to be the son of an esteemed military general like her father.

According to her father, Major Khushwant Ranjan, if you did not belong to a military family or did not have a stand-up on your own feet, with at least half a crore yearly package, you had no right whatsoever to even hallucinate about his daughter.

This was her father's notion for the past three years, and now of his complaisant daughter for the past three weeks.

I answered the call. An apprehensive voice came from the other side,

"Hello! Hello! ...am I talking to Ajay Singh Thakur?"

"Yes, I am. Who's this?" I said in a comatose voice.

"Sir, I am Kabir, your uncle's accountant and secretary. I have been working with him for two months. You might remember Mr Prakash who had served him for the last twenty years as his account manager."

I said, "Yes, definitely! How can I forget him! Prakash Ji has been always very fond of me. Is he retired now?"

The reply staggered me. "He is no more, sir. He passed away two months ago. *He was my father.*"

"Oh!... I'm...I'm so sorry. It's so sad to hear. He was backbone to my uncle. Uncle took every decision after taking his advice..."

Kabir interrupted me, "Sir, he would be glad if you can come to see him immediately. It is very urgent."

"Come what!" I was startled. "What's the matter? Is he alright?"

"Sir, he wishes not to let you know anything until you arrive. And well, he is not rather alright. He had a cardiac arrest and was in hospital for the last one week. He has been shifted to his mansion today as he refused to stay any longer in hospital. Doctors have commended him not to talk much. That's why he authorized me to call you."

"But I need to finish some important work over here," I lied. I had not left my apartment since three weeks and the very fancy of getting out was nightmarish.

He replied, "Sir, pardon me but he does not have much time left, that's what he told me to convey."

I was dazed. "The reason he left the hospital was because he wants to spend his last days in his mansion."

Without any second thought, I replied, "Inform uncle that I will be there as soon as possible." He was rejoiced to hear that, "That's very nice to hear sir. Just let me know the time of your arrival and I will be there personally to receive you. Good bye."

As soon as the call ended, Rahim entered the room. On seeing the pieces of broken glass and scattered milk, he asked "Baba, how did it happen?"

"Oh Rahim, I was probing for my phone while I was half asleep when I accidently meddled with the glass lying beside it."

"Beside your phone? But, I remember correctly that I had kept it on your study table just ten minutes ago."

I was a bit amazed. My study table was at the other corner of the room, and Rahim was a man with a very sharp memory. He could not have been erroneous.

"And what did you say? You were looking for your phone at this late hour!"

I said, "Rahim, uncle's new secretary called from Jaisinghpur. He is serious. I need to visit him urgently. I think I'll leave by the first flight tomorrow morning to Delhi, and then catch a bus from there to Jaisinghpur."

On hearing this, Rahim's face turned pale. "What happened to Raj Singh Ji?"

"He had a heart attack a few days ago. It's a pity that I have come to know about it so late."

"Ajay baba, you are very well aware of my fealty toward him. You might not like what I am going to say, but..." he hesitated "...accepting an invite along with a *glass-break*, is considered in my village to be very sinister. I appeal you not to go!"

"Rahim!" I screamed at him. "Are you out of your senses? Do you realize what are you speaking? How can you talk like this, despite the fact that he deems you as his most allegiant man?"

"I know baba what I am speaking, my fidelity toward him is indubitable. I apologize if my absurdity hurt you."

"That's alright. Now, please pack my bag for tomorrow, I am going online to book air ticket to Delhi."

Rahim said, "I apologize again baba, if you felt bad."

He turned around, "But, I did not keep the glass besides your phone," and left the room.

I felt very bad for hurting him, as Rahim had been taking care of me since my childhood. He was the most entrusted man of my uncle who had been there for me since I lost my mother.

I booked my flight ticket to Delhi for the next day and finished my dinner. Now, I think I shall sleep again, so that tomorrow I shall start the day without any residual hangover.

Anjana's Last Email to Ajay
October 5, 2010 (three weeks ago)

Hi Ajay, I hope that this mail finds you in high spirits. I had been diligently calling you for the past one week, but each time you failed to respond. Hence, I am conveying my sentiments through this mail.

I know the last time we met, it ended on a vexed note. I really felt very denigrated on the day when you came to my house with your proposal to meet my father. The way he insulted you apathetically really shattered me. But, you left suddenly and did not give me a chance to display my tears that continued well past the next morning.

In my entire lifetime, I have never sobbed so much before, hope you trust that.

Ajay, what I am going to convey, shall make you hate me for the entire life, and I know that I deserve it as well.

First of all, I want to make one thing very crystal. This has got nothing to do with anyone being settled abroad or belonging to a stupid idolized family. These are the last things on earth that would ever entertain me, you know it very well.

I want to share with you my intent of doing so, if you care to understand. As you are aware that my mother died during my birth, however my father never made me feel that gap in my life. He has rightfully fulfilled his duties as a parent, and played the role of both mother and father to me.

He never remarried for my sake although he was young when my mother passed away. He never wanted a stepmother who might create differences in his mind against me.

He did all that but never asserted anything in return. But now, he appealed me of something. He clamored me to get settled where he believes is a more fitting place.

I did not know what to reply. I tried hard to convince him this entire week, but he would not listen. Instead, he was so much firm on his will that he resorted to fast until death.

On the other hand, Ajay, you didn't reply to me either.

I hope you will understand why I did so. I cannot build my acropolis of love on my father's grave. What beatitude would come out of that?

Hence, I had to submit to him.

I am getting engaged in four days and will marry probably by the end of this month.

I know that you will never forgive me, but I want you to acknowledge why I did so. Please never forget all those wonderful and nostalgic moments we cherished together in the last three years, as I shall not, until my last breath.

May be god has better plans for us in the next life.

Forever yours,

Anju. ☹☹☹

Excerpts from "New Jaipur Times"
Jaisinghpur–October 19, 2009 (a year ago)

Jatin Mehta steel company , plans to set up a new plant in alliance with the Rajasthan government in Jaisinghpur, a small town near Jaipur. It shall become the fourth largest steel manufacturing unit in India. The company had some trouble in acquiring the land, like previous incidents in Nandi gram and Singur. There was a group of farmers still despondent with the reimbursement. But later, there seemed to be a decent concord between them. Overall, it was a smooth ride for Mehta and his company. Work over it starts the next month.

Jaisinghpur–August 22, 2010 (two months ago)

Two days ago, three laborers were found to be missing from their quarters near the plant. Till now, it has not been possible to locate their whereabouts. Police have discovered few blood stains in their room. Samples have been sent for forensic analysis. Rajesh Singh, Superintendent of Police, is supposed to release a statement once the analysis report comes. The other laborers are in a state of terror.

Jaisinghpur–August 27, 2010 (two months ago)
Rajesh Singh's Press Statement

"Regarding astraying of the three men, police is working hard and shall soon find clues about them. As per the forensic report, the blood stains obtained in the room might belong to the missing men. However, another set of blood was found, which could not be identified as human. By far, police has come to a preliminary assumption that it may be a case of any animal attack. People are advised to be careful, to keep their doors locked properly at night."

"Mr. Singh, is there a contingency of human involvement in their disappearance? Last week, there was a commotion between the company and some laborers. They purported that management is not providing them elementary amenities and choking them to work over long hours without substantial increment in salary," one of the journalists asked.

"I do not have any clue regarding that. I shall probe into the matter and only after that can opine upon it. And yes, as of now, there is any feasibility in this case. We'll let you know as soon as any new info is annexed to us."

CHAPTER 2

SAWMYA

Ajay's Diary
October 26, 2010–8 pm

After getting stuck in the infamous Delhi traffic for three damn hours, I finally arrived at the ISBT bus stand at Kashmiri gate almost two hours ago from the airport. The roadway authorities told that there is only one bus remaining for Jaisinghpur. I had food at a local canteen at the bus stand itself called *'Dilli Dhaba.'*

While I was about to conclude the third paneer paratha, a beautiful damsel came to me and asked "Excuse me, is anybody coming here?" denoting the chair next to mine.

She was one of the most amazingly attractive women I had ever seen in my life. Even Anjana was fleckless, but this girl standing in front of me took my breath away.

At that moment, I realized the essence of the lyrics I had heard years ago in a Tom Cruise movie, *'Take my breath away.'* Her hair was midnight-black and it flowed over her shoulders. Her lips appeared as honey sweet. She had a wine glass shaped waist wrapped in a bright pink salwar suit and a complexion that could lit up the bus stand, in case of any electrical failure; and not to overlook, her hazel eyes, so vibrant with life.

She repeated, "Excuse me, are you ok?" I came back to my senses. "Oh yes... it is vacant."

"Sorry to bother you. I know there are other tables idle, but it is not okay in this city for a girl to be seen alone anywhere, let lone a public place." She continued, "I've had such issues earlier in the past. People here predicate a lonely good looking girl to be public property."

Not only was she exceedingly alluring, she was exceedingly aware of it too.

I said, "I comply with you. I have read in newspapers about inflation in crimes happening to young women in Delhi. I assume it ranks one of the highest in our country. Even Mumbai, where I stay is safer when it comes to security of women traveling alone in night."

I had extirpated the paratha, but it was still half an hour for the bus to depart and virtuously speaking, I could not have left her alone.

She introduced herself to me.Her name was Sawmya. She had completed her MA in political science at Lady Sri Ram College, Delhi and had been tabbed as a reporting journalist in one of the prominent English news channels. I could prevision the TRP of the news channel rocketing the sky, as everybody would love to watch this beautiful and mesmerizing journalist every night.

Her first assignment was going to begin in three weeks and she was going to Jaisinghpur to visit her aunt with whom she stayed during the early years of school before turning temperatures of Delhi high. Her parents had died in a train accident while she was a child. Her aunt was a school teacher, who did not marry in order to take care of her parentless niece.

Bizarre, but true, all this she narrated in our very first meet!

"So you too are going to Jaisinghpur, which means that I have the privilege of escorting you in the bus too," I tried best to hide my wicked smile, unsuccessfully.

She smiled back, "Well, of course, if you do not mind. Actually, I was supposed to catch the bus much earlier in day time, but got held up due to some damn assignment. I have never done a night journey alone before, so it would be fabulous if you can accompany me. You know it's not inviolable even in the bus, as most of the crowd going to Jaisinghpur is local suburban. And these men do not demur to grope a girl while asleep, here and there. You know what I mean."

I said in my mind, 'Well, if I sit next to you, while you are asleep, then more than other men it would be me who has to restrain not to touch you here and there.'

"Of course, as I said, it would be my privilege." She gave even a cuter smile this time.

Till a while back, I was an amateur chronic alcoholic about to turn pro, because of the *'breakup with Anjana'* episode, and now all of a sudden I was feverish like a teenager. *A sign of typical bipolar disorder* (any qualified psychiatrist would tell you that). I took excuse from her saying that I have to write some important notes in my diary, and I believe all I have scrawled, *is about her.*

Ajay's Diary
October 27, 2010–2 pm

It has been a wondrous day! The bus arrived at seven in the morning at Jaisinghpur. Kabir, himself came to receive me. He was a young man, almost of my age. Well-built and at six-feet height, he inherited all the lineaments of his deceased father. However, let me continue with the night earlier. As soon as the bus engine ignited, Sawmya asked, "Do you stay in Jaisinghpur or have any drill over there? You see, I have apprised too much about myself back there. Now, I shall just listen."

Well, I was alright with her chattering! "I am going there to visit my uncle. Since few days, he is not in a good health. Actually, the last time I went there was almost four years ago. I was five years old when my father left my mother and me, since then he has buttressed me emotionally and financially." "Oh! Sorry to know about your father. I realize how it feels to lose your parent at a very young age; you see I lost both of mine."

"Don't be sorry, he is probably still alive. He did not leave the world; instead he left our world for the world of another woman."

My words startled her. "What? Oh! I am sorry again... I mean, who was that woman?" "As I said, I was probably five years old, I did not understand anything then. Moreover, my mother passed away in the years to come. Later, I was brought up by my uncle. Neither he told me much about it nor did I try to enquire about my father. After all, he was and is still as good as dead for me."

I hushed for a few minutes, none of us spoke. "When I think about it, I feel irated, as he left behind a woman, mentally broken, and a child fatherless."

I was silent again, this time for few seconds though. "My mother went into severe depression. She was put on loads of anti-depressants. And finally, one night, overdose of those pills took depression away from her life, forever. I was ten then." And then I could not speak any further.

The scene of my mother lying placid that morning came alive like a ghost in front of me. I had no idea why she was sleeping so long; normally otherwise she would wake me up, prepare my breakfast, and accompany me to the school bus.

I left for school without breakfast that day. When I returned in the afternoon, she was still lying in the same manner. I called up my neighbor uncle, who after touching my mother's body immediately dialed up simultaneously the ambulance and the police. I was not able to make out what did he feel on touching her. The *'white dressed people'* who came in the ambulance did some tests on her that I could not comprehend. They parted away her eyelids and casted torch light on the eyes.

I heard one of them saying, *'pupil is not reactive'* and then *'I cannot find any pulse,' 'body is in rigor mortis... it's already been a few hours since death,' 'I am sorry she is dead.'*

'Dead!' that was the first term I understood among of all the medical terminologies. I realized what had happened. My mother too left me. But not for another man, like my father.

She left because she didn't have one. Then, I touched her for the first time that day. It was something very diacritic about the touch. It was cold. The touch felt cold. Not just cold, extremely cold. She was dead, she was cold!

'Dead are cold.' Not just cold, *'Dead are extremely cold'!* This I learned that day at the age of ten.

Suddenly, I was startled. The touch had become warm.

Warm? But she was dead! How could it be warm? I woke up from my dream. It was Sawmya's hand touching mine.

"Hey! Are you lost? I'm so sorry to hear about your mother." Her hand was so warm that I felt life plunging back in me.

"Thanks for listening. Anyways, let's talk about something else." I told her about my uncle. "He is my mother's elder and only brother. He has no family of his own. He has been taking care of me since then. Initially, I lived a few years there with him. Later, he got me admission in one of the best-boarding schools in the country and also to the finest college. Today, I live in Mumbai in a luxurious apartment, I have a genuine caretaker, and it is all because of his generosity. However, I feel I have not done enough for him."

"So how long are you going to stay there?" she asked.

"Don't know. According to his doctors, he is not going to live much longer. Therefore, I believe this time I shall make up for my negligence toward him as long as he is alive."

"Oh! It's sad to know." The way she said 'Oh!' made her look very cute. There was nothing pretentious in her. She had a sense of empathy every time she said that.

"And you are going back to Delhi in three weeks for your new job? Must be very exciting?"

"Actually I've already begun my first job assignment. My first documentary is about the recent happenings in Jaisinghpur. For that I am going to garner enough material before officially working on it."

I asked cluelessly, "Recent happenings! What's going on there?"

"Don't you read newspapers or watch television? Don't you know what's going on there? News about that place is everywhere now a days."

It was true. In the last few days, since Anjana's turndown, I had completely withdrawn into my apartment. I did not meet anyone, did not turn on the television or peeped into the newspapers.

I had arrived at the conviction that without Anjana, the whole world had collapsed for me, hence there was no point in knowing what was happening in it. I even thought of suicide as a decent option to put an end to my misery but somehow did not have the audacity to do so.

She continued further without advertising any more surprise over my nescience.

"There have been a lot of people reported missing from the place. It all started two months earlier with astraying of three laborers who were working in a newly launched steel factory. Earlier, everybody thought that due to some domestic conflict over demands by the labor union, it was the management behind it. However, it did not just stop there. Very soon, people from other places were found to be missing as well who had absolutely nothing to do with the factory.

And soon people discovered the horrible." She paused again; I waited again, this time with no patience.

"What?"

"Their bodies were discovered in a mutilated condition, with their heads twisted around and feet turned backward. "

I said in a shocked state "What? Head turned around and....! Who the hell on earth could do that?"

"I have been frequently visiting this place, because I was worried about my aunt. She says that all of the incidents happened only during the night time. If you shut your doors and stay in your house in the night, you are absolutely safe."

"Who is responsible for that? I mean, it's really frightful!"

"Yes, it is. And that's why I am going there, to sift the truth behind the crime. That's what a journalist does, right?" she asked and answered at the same time.

I nodded affirmatively, I had to!

We further spoke about the incidents and other things till late night. I did not realize when I slept. When I woke up, I had arrived at my destination. The screeching of bus tires woke me up like the cock-a-a-doodle-doo in the dawn.

"Hey, good morning!" Sawmya cheered.

I could not exactly say about the morning being good or not, but at least after days, I finally witnessed a morning that otherwise had become as abstracted as Anjana.

"Good morning to you too." By the time I replied she had pulled off her traveling bag on her slender shoulders and climbed out of the bus. I hurriedly took my luggage and exited out too.

As soon as she got down, all the auto wallas surrounded her. They all begged her to come with them. I managed to spear the mob and get closer to her.

"Shall I accompany you till your place?" I asked her, wondering if in case she was irked by them.

"It's okay. You have patrolled me like an angel the entire night. I must thank you a lot for that." She chuckled, "Now I will manage from here."

I was about to ask her contact number, when I felt a tap on my left shoulder. I turned around.

"Hello sir, I guess you are Mr Ajay!" A young man standing behind me said.

"I am. You must be Kabir!"

"Yes sir, I am. Kindly hand over to me your bag."

By the time I turned around, Sawmya had already left.

CHAPTER 3

DEAD ON ARRIVAL

Ajay's Diary (continued)

U ncle was very frantic to see me. He exclaimed, "Ajay, it has been ages since I have seen you! Come, come closer to me!" He embraced me for a long time. "For a while after I had this heart attack, I thought that I may not be able to see you in this flimsy life again. God's grace you have come. Now, I can die harmoniously at last."

I replied, not without the guilt of not frequenting him in the last couple of years, "Uncle, how can I not come to visit you in this terrible condition of yours, knowing very well that you always have stood behind me like a bedrock? If I would have not had you in my life, I don't know what it would have been like."

"Come on dear! What have I done for you? Nothing! Your mother was my little sister and you are like my son. You know that I have no family of my own. For whom does a man earns. To cater his family a good life. You and your mother were the only family I had, and with your mother gone, the only person left is you. Leave that aside, you must be fatigued due to the journey. You better go to your room and take some rest. I shall meet you at the lunch. We have lots to canvass, for which I have summoned you."

"Ok uncle, you better take rest too, will see you later."

I left his room and marched toward mine downstairs. He had preserved my room in the same state as when I used to stay here. I better take some rest now; felt very gratulated to converse with him after ages.

Ajay's Diary
October 27, 2010–11.45 pm

After lying on the bed, I don't remember when sleep overwhelmed me. I slept like a horse. It was around one o' clock when Ram veer woke me up. He was my uncle's housekeeper for the past twenty-five years.

"Baba, Sahib is waiting for you in the dining hall." I rose up and in a half-conscious state and went to the hall. There, I found uncle sitting at the very end of a long dining table. I sat at the other end, straight opposite to him. The food on the table was lavish, as always in his mansion. It looked like an unlimited buffet of a five-star hotel that included all kinds of saliva-stimulating dishes ever invented on this earth. I could not help myself but to gormandize at the table. A few more days in the phase that I was going through in my apartment; satiating my stomach with nothing but alcohol, I would have given Christian Bale a good run for his money if the producers of *The Machinist* were conspiring a sequel.

Next to uncle was Kabir standing, with folded hands. Kabir truly reflected his father in every aspect. "What can I get for you, sir?" he asked uncle. "Get me one scotch. Large, with ice, as always."

I said without hesitating for a moment, "Pardon me, uncle, but you just had a heart attack! You should not have any alcohol at all!"

"Look my son, if my time has come to go, then nothing can roadblock it. Neither any doctors nor anything else.

Therefore, it does not matter, a drink or two. Anyways, I have called you so far to discuss something very important." He paused for a moment. Kabir was there instantly with his drink.

He took a sip of the scotch, and then continued, "As you are well aware of the fact that I do not have anybody behind me to gander after all these assets when I am gone, except you. Therefore, I think that it is the right time for you to take charge while I am still alive. So that, I shall die in peace when the moment comes, also assured that all I have amassed in my entire life is in the right hands."

"Please uncle, kindly don't say a word about you dying or so. You are here to live for many more years to come. And regarding the inheritance of your property, I do not think I am the right person for all of this. I consider myself too crude to take this burden as of now," I replied.

"Ajay that's too generous of you to say so. I know that you are gifted of handling any charge given to you. Besides, there is Kabir, whom I trust the most, after his father, Prakash. He will always stand with you in every circumstance, good or bad. Isn't it Kabir?" Uncle looked at him in a dual catechizing and affirmatory manner.

"Definitely sir, it is my honor to serve you. Only due to your patronage to my father, he could send me to school and later to college. I shall never embitter you in any circumstance," Kabir said.

"But, uncle, I am not yet arranged..." he cut me off.

"I don't want to hear any further Ajay. If you want to do any favor to me then do not dither. *It is my last disposition.* Does that mean anything to you?"

"It does not mean *anything*; it means *everything* to me uncle. It's just that I don't know how am I going to handle all of your establishments, as I am just a postgraduate student in Arts. I don't have any kind of inwardness in management."

"Dear, don't you know my educational background? I did not even complete high school. It is not the college education that makes a person capable. An adroit is either born adroit or he makes himself so by his instinctive nature. I know you have that aptitude, whether you believe in it or not. I have not grown old without being able to diagnose that trait in a person."

He paused again to take a sip of his scotch and continued, "As you are aware that I have a textile mill that is the most important possession of my life. However, I want you to go tomorrow and have a foretaste of the charitable hospital and the school that I am running for the past five years. That is where my main interest lies. Not in terms of money, but the service what I have tried to do to the people of this place. Also, once I am no more, I do not want any fraudulency in the name of charity."

And so, he went on, diagramming me of his various others endowments, his unfulfilled emulations, his expectations of me almost until midnight; after which I went back to my room. As I was lying on my bed, I was thinking how life takes turmoil sometimes so suddenly. Till yesterday, I was *no nobody guy* to whom a father did not want his daughter to get married. Today, I have almost become the wealthiest man; at least of this town. Despite that, I was not any degree glad. To me, luxuriance meant all those times when I would buy Anjana an unworthy present, which elated her. Here, I laid in my bed; *affluent and alone.*

Ajay's Diary

October 28, 2010–7 pm

What a long and exhilarating day! After breakfast, I left with Kabir to the hospital. It is merely five kilometers from uncle's house. However, I must correct myself. In this small town, everything is 'merely' close to each other. On arrival, the first thing I noticed in the hospital was its board.

'Jaisinghpur Seva Hospital'

Of the few charitable hospitals that I came across, I recorded that all of them were named after one's deceased parents or close ones. But uncle probably had his reasons for not having done so. Even I had little knowledge about my maternal grandparents, except for the fact that my great-grandfather was a landlord of this town, when once it was a village. Those were the times before independence. Then, everything changed. It evolved from a village to a suburb town that it is now today.

"Welcome sir!" I was greeted with a garland and sweets by the staff of the hospital. There were few nursing people, two young doctors, and some ward staff among them.

The 'white dressed people'!

They had been waiting for me since early morning. They took me to a relatively large room above which was engraved *'Director's Chamber.'*

"Sir, please be seated. Get a cup of tea for sir," an old nurse directed the ward boy.

I said, "How can I sit here? It is my uncle's chair. And, he still is the director of the hospital."

Kabir came ahead, "Very true sir, he indeed is. And very soon, you are going to be the bearer of this chair. Your uncle shall be august to see you occupy it. That's what he yearns for."

"Ok then." I sat down on the chair, feeling extremely flustered, as I knew that I did not deserve that position and I also never received a VIP treatment earlier in my life.

Once I entired the tea, one of the two doctors; *Dr. Nirmal* (as was printed on his apron badge) said, "Sir, would you like to have a lap of the hospital? I believe it is your first visit."

"Certainly!" It was a kind of antic, as I had never even been to a medical college in my life, and today I am supposed to be running a hospital.

"This is our general ward, sir. It is forty bedded. There are currently thirty-three patients admitted."

"Good," I nodded. *I was not sure what I meant when I did so.*

Then, we moved up to the private-ward lobby and entered into one of them. In that room, there was an old patient lying motionless on the bed. Our influx did not seem to bother his half-conscious state.

"Sir, these are the best private wards we have in the town," the doctor cheered. It was indeed a good one, almost like the ones we had in cities.

While moving out, it suddenly appeared to me as if I had seen that old man somewhere before. I could not recollect when and where?

I asked Dr. Nirmal, "Who is that patient and what has happened to him?"

"He is the father of SP police, Rajesh Singh. You must have heard about him. He is the most defiant and honorable policeman this town has ever seen. His father recently got an attack of paralysis. It's so tragic that it happened to him. He himself is a very earnest man and a noble school teacher. He has led his entire life in a pious fashion, and has raised his son to be an honest and inspiring police officer."

By then,we arrived in front of the OT complex.

"This is our Operation Theatre (OT). We have two tables of general anesthesia and one full-time anesthetist. Do you want to have a look inside? You have to put on the OT gown and slippers in order to maintain sterility."

"Oh no, it is alright. I do not have much time today. I have to visit other places too." The actuality was that I was damn scared of the operation theatres. The very fancy of someone putting a knife on a man's skin (let alone be it a surgical knife and the patient not feeling an inch of pain) was terrifying to me.

Then, near the theatre was one large machine in separate room whose even name I didn't understood.

"This is the autoclave, sir. Here is where all theatre instruments are sterilized."

"I know about that one," was my reflex reply, despite having heard that term for the first time. Next, we were supposed to go further up to the ICU, when a nurse came running toward Dr. Nirmal. She murmured something in his ears.

His facial expression changed suddenly to an appalled one.

"What happened doctor?" I asked.

"Well sir, I have to attend the Emergency Room(ER)."

"Is there a casualty? I'll come with you. I too want to see the ER."

"You can come sir, if you insist. But keep your heart strong. There are some things which might not be painless to see."

I followed the doctor to the ER. There was quite a cluster of people around a trolley. I was not able to visualize the patient on trolley distinctly. One of the nursing staff shouted, "Please go outside everybody except one or two with the victim, doctor Sahib has arrived."

"Victim! Of what?" was the flash of thought that ran through my head. I was athirst to know what happened to that 'victim.' Murder? Rape? Accident? Suicide? *Or was he a victim of betrayal in love, like me?*

I noticed that there were two policemen too in that crowd, which now was about to disperse.

When the arena was relatively clear, I saw a middle-aged man lying on the trolley. He seemed to be well built and nourished. The doctor put his stethoscope on the left side of the man's chest and waited for about ten seconds before announcing, "There is no heartbeat! Get the ECG machine quickly!"

I could not figure out what was the cause of his death, as I could see no signs of trauma on his body. Although, there was something different about him.

And then, it struck to me!

And my jaw dropped dead when it did!!

I actually did not believe Sawmya when she told me in the bus the previous night, *'and soon their bodies were found with their head and feet turned backward.'* But it was true and that eerie truth laid in front of me on the trolley.

The man's head and feet were twisted backward! Dr. Nirmal himself applied the ECG leads. I marveled whether there was any use of it now, as that guy could not have been alive in that condition! May be he needed to complete the protocol to assure that there was no sign of vitality left. On clicking one button on the machine, the paper began to stir with appearance of few black lines running in a dead straight manner on a pink paper.

'Pupil is not reactive'

'I cannot find any pulse'

'body is in rigor mortis'

'it's already been a few hours since death, ECG is flat. Sorry she is dead.' Those words again screamed in my head.

I felt a bit of dizziness and sat down on a chair nearby.

Dr. Nirmal told the nurse standing beside him, "Sister, declare him dead. *Dead on arrival.*"

"Sir, are you alright?" asked Kabir who had been silent all this time.

"I am ok, I think I need some fresh air."

"Sure sir, let us go outside." He accompanied me outside the emergency room gate. In the lobby outside, there was now a large assemblage. In addition to the people who already were earlier with the victim, now there were many more. Most of them did not seem to be related to the victim, but had an element more of snoopiness rather than concernment. There were two policemen whom I saw earlier inside. *And then, there she was. Sawmya!*

That was the first sigh of relief I had in the last twenty minutes.

She was interrogating the policeman with her questions.

"Where was this body recovered? Whom do you think is behind all these murders? Why is not the police doing anything in arresting the criminals?" I think they were paying more attention to her features rather than her questions. And then, one of them spoke.

"Listen madam, all of your questions will be answered by SP Sahib. And the body was found by the local people near the *'kaala jungle.'* We do not have any details to furnish any further on this."

That was the time I poked Sawmya. She turned around and was amazed to see me.

"Hi, what a surprise! How come you are here? Was that victim agnated to you?"

"No, no! Not at all! I will tell you when you are done with your Q&A session and find some time for... I suppose... late breakfast!"

"Oh sure! Anyway, these policemen do not seem to be replying anything accordingly. So where are you taking me out?"

Next voice was that of Kabir. "Sir, you can go to a nearby restaurant just behind the hospital. It has a very good name for nice fast food. I will wait for you here in the car."

"It would have been better if you could come with us," I said.

"Definitely sir, but I have some important phone calls to make. I shall disturb your conversation."

I liked him for that.

He indeed was a smart man with a good presence of mind.

"So what do you like to have?"

"Hmm"... She said looking briskly at the menu, "I will have a coffee and cheese sandwich."

I said to the waiter who was standing with folded hands and a big mustache. "Please get a coffee, cheese sandwich for the lady and tea for me."

"Just a tea? That's pretty miser as compared to a girl's order!"

"Actually, I had a heavy breakfast at my uncle's house. I do not even feel like eating anything till evening. So how is your dissection going on? It was very awful to see that body back there. Do you have any lead into *who is* behind this heinous act?"

"Not yet. Though I have read about such kind of murders somewhere long ago, I cannot recollect about it. I think that somebody is trying to terrify the people. May be a psychopath or a bunch of them."

"Madam, your sandwich and coffee, and sir, your tea," interrupted the waiter.

She continued after taking a bite of the delicious looking sandwich and a sip of coffee, "Let us talk about something else. How is your uncle?"

"He is fine. His doctors have a different assessment; although he does not give a damn about what they have advised. He is assigning all his amenabilities to my shoulders and I am very fidgety; whether I'll be able to fit in his shoes or not. The probability of latter seems more vivid at the moment."

"Oh! You should not disesteem yourself. If he has laid this burden upon you, he must have thought it adequately before doing so. I enquired about your uncle. He is indeed not only a wealthy person, but a genuine human being too. Ok! So that's the reason why you were there at the hospital. It belongs to him, right? And now to you!"

"That's true, but as I told you I am more nervous than excited about it. On that note, I forgot that I also have to visit the school and then, the textile mill. I should leave now. I will call you later. So when are we meeting again?"

"May be tomorrow afternoon. And to call me you need to have my number," she said meekly. "Oops, sorry... so what's your number?"

I left after taking her number followed by a visit to the school and the mill. They too were exhaustive ones, making me more ambiguous whether acceding to uncle was a prudent decision. As I mentioned in the start, it was a long and exhilarating day but forgot to underline, a damn taxing too. And yes, I did call Sawmya and am going to meet her tomorrow again. Same place. Good night.

CHAPTER 4

IT'S A WITCH BEHIND THE MURDERS!

Ajay's Diary –
October 29, 2010–11 pm

What a great conflict of beliefs a human mind can have in just a short period, is hard to digest! It began as an alight day, like a reverie; but as it matured, it turned to be a dark and gloomy one.

"So how were your sojourns yesterday, Ajay? I hope that you liked them. I am sorry, I was busy in stacking some official documents by the time you arrived; hence could not meet you," uncle inquisited over the breakfast table.

"It was great uncle. Though everything was neoteric to me, but I think I will get used to them as an assignee under your auspices and Kabir's aid."

"Well said! However, there is one more thing, which I failed to inform you yesterday. I advise you not to be outside alone in this town after dark. By now, you would have already heard about the atrocious murders that have recently taken place. Kabir posted me about yesterday's casualty at the hospital."

"But uncle, who do you think is behind these dreaded murders? I've never heard of such acts of monstrosity ever before."

"Dear Ajay, history is full of such acts of monstrosity; may be of dissimilar genre. Haven't you heard of the Nithari case in which innocent children were killed and their body parts eaten by a lunatic? Or that incident, when a schizoid roasted his wife in a tandoor. This world is studded with such psychopaths who in order to satisfy their absurd lust can do anything. What is happening in this town is another stereotype of that. And to add flavor, there are these half-witted anecdotes what people here are breeding."

"What anecdotes?"

"Didn't you read today's local newspaper; the story of yesterday's murder? Well then..." he fondled his hands under the breakfast table, "... here it is, read the front page."

Excerpt from–JAISINGHPUR NAVCHETANA
October 29, 2010
IT'S A WITCH BEHIND THE MURDERS!

Yet another murder took place the night earlier. Narayan Lal aged thirty-two, a farmer by occupation, was found dead in a well near the *kaala jungle* (or the *black forest*). In the similar manner as the earlier murders, his neck and feet were twisted.

The police have landed in utter failure in their job to find the murderer, as this is the eleventh straight murder in just two months.

However, this time, there is a witness of the cold-blooded act. Manohar Das, aged thirty-eight, another farmer claims that he saw Narayan pursuing *a witch* the night before. Here is his exclusive interview to our newspaper:

"I was returning to my home from the field yesterday night on my cycle, when I saw Narayan walking clueless toward the kaala jungle. I tried to stop him and probe where he was wandering in the middle of the night, as his home was in an opposite direction. But he did not respond and continued to walk. *Then I saw her.* He was following a woman. She was wearing a kind of bridal dress, but *it was black in color!* I could not see her face distinctly as it was covered with her long hair and it was a cloudy night. At first, I thought that she was a whore who had convinced Narayan to follow her to the jungle. But when I looked down at her, I was shocked to the core. *Her feet were turned backward! She was a witch!! She was a witch!!* Only a witch can have feet turned backward. And then I realized. The witch had cast a spell on him and he was following her under some kind of hypnotism to the forest, where she could perform her misdeed on him. There was no other option left for me rather to run away, or else I would have become another victim at her hands.

I was so scared that I went straight to my home. I immediately closed the doors and shut off the lights, as I feared that the witch might follow me to my home. Today morning, I came to know what was expected. Now, I fear for my life because one who has seen the witch does not stay alive for a long time.

She will hunt me down and kill me the way she killed Narayan and the others. Hence, I am planning to leave this place along with my family very soon."

So is there a witch in town? Are all the abominable acts done by a witch?

We asked these questions to SP police, Rajesh Singh, who replied almost in an affronted manner. "That's an utter humbug! There is no entity called *witch* not only in this town, but anywhere in this world. This is just a fantasy of these cockamamie and feeble-minded people. I know that the police have not been able to pin down the culprits yet, but we are very close in doing so. However, as of now, I cannot disclose any information. But, I assure you that very soon the scoundrels shall be arrested and castigated."

On finishing the article, I said, "This is total absurdity. A witch! Don't the people have any better rumors to spread? What is your opinion regarding this uncle?"

"What can I say? I have seen this place ripening from merely a village to a suburb that it is today; all due to the hard work and dauntlessness of its people. And these incidents lately have dragged it nearly hundred years back when people used to attribute every ill happening in the neighborhood to some kind of witchcraft or tantrism.

The only promise to this town is young lads like you, who can annihilate these myths that were once so rampant in our society. Anyway, enough with this stuff, I think you should leave now. It will take a couple of days before getting into the skin of ventures, which you soon shall be heading; that are so different all together."

I left with Kabir. Today's visit was to an automobile workshop that too belongs to uncle.

'What's left in this world where he is not involved?' I asked myself.

While we were taking a round of the workshop, Kabir got a call from the mill.

After finishing the call he said, "Sir, there is a small issue at the mill. One of the machines has jammed, and I have to quickly go there to supervise.

You may come with me if you wish or else you can finish the visit over here, as the mess can be fixed by me alone."

I replied, "I think Kabir; you can leave for the mill. I will continue here."

"Ok sir, I will call you once I am done with the work," and he left.

The real motive in sending him to the mill alone was that I could wrap up my visit in the automobile shop quickly and catch up with Sawmya soon.

And so we were there in the same restaurant behind the hospital an hour later. "One cheese sandwich and coffee please... hmm! What else do you have?... one masala dosa too... and what do you like to have?" she ordered to the waiter and asked me in one go.

"I'll have the same too. "

She was looking a lot prettier than the first time we met. Her purple salwar suit fit to the body, displaying every curve of her with the matching dupatta was a perfect menu for the eyes.

Being with her were the only hang-loose times I cherished since my arrival in the town.

"So how was your latter half of yesterday? I mean your visit to the school and mill?"

"Well, it was fine. And to mention about the automobile workshop I visited just before coming here."

"Did you read today's newspaper? The story of yesterday's murder?"

I was not expecting to take off today's 'kind-of-a-date' with her with same eerie talks that I already had with uncle during breakfast.

"Yes, I did. What to do you think is the truth behind this story? That man, what is his name? Manohar. Is he simply maligning for publicity or did he really sight something?"

"I have already met him." I was stunned by her astuteness. "I told him that I was a journalist from a national news network and would defray a decent sum if he recounts the previous night. And you know what? He is hardly interested in any publicity or money. He told me that there is nothing to append to what he had already disclosed to the 'Navchetana' guys. He was busy talking to somebody regarding taking care of his farm till he comes back and shouting at his wife for the delay in packing the household items. That poor chap is really cocksure of his delusion and is planning his way to flee the place as soon as possible."

"Are you also convinced of his story?"

"No, I am not. As I said it was his misapprehension. However, it should also be inquisited what did he see that night? Whether Narayan was seen with a woman by anyone else? The police has not even approached him for taking his statement. They said to me that Manohar might be drunk that night and so espied what he did in his deluded state. It is not the first time that someone has reported seeing a witch or a ghost. People have often claimed to have seen aliens. Most of them were later found to be under the effect of some kind of hallucinogen."

"The police may be righteous as well. But why is he then trying to elope? His delusion or hallucination or whatever it is, seems to have costed him too much."

"I cannot say anything regarding that. The only thing I am concerned is the timing of his statement. Amidst of the events that have taken place in the town lately, it may bound to have a derogatory impact on the state of mind of its residents. Anyway, let us not irk ourselves any further. Why don't you visit my house? I mean my aunt's house, where I am staying. I can make you a better tea then what you had here or anywhere else. And dinner too, if you can stay till then."

"Definitely! I have already finished my timetable for the day."

It was a broad lie. I was docked to go to one more place along with Kabir.

I called up and convinced him to narrate some fancy story to uncle of our being stuck up somewhere and that we shall return late to the mansion.

As Don Corleone would have quoted *'she made me an offer, I can't refuse.'*

Her house was about seven kilometers from the restaurant, quite a hefty distance in the town. It was an old farmhouse settled another kilometer off NH-8.

Her aunt opened the door. She had an impassive face and appeared older enough to be her grandmother rather than an aunt, carrying perhaps twenty years extra on her shoulders.

"Sawmi, where had you been? I tried your cell phone number endlessly. It is not that safe to be out after dusk. You are already sentient of the witch, who is hunting people after dark; it is better to stay in the house rather than investing your life at risk."

"Dear aunt, do not worry. Nothing shall happen to your brave little niece. And it is much safer to be out in this town after dark whether there is *'a witch or no witch'* rather to be out in the city where I live and travel each day. Now, if you kindly permit, shall we come inside?"

"Sure, sure," she opened the door in entirety and as she did, her eyes buckled on me for the first time.

She glanced at me in a queer fashion, similar to a father who is suddenly taken aback when her daughter enters home one find day with her boyfriend. "He is Ajay. Remember, I told you about him? The same guy who accompanied me in the bus. He has come to visit his uncle and is likely to stay here for a long time. " I noticed her keeping that smile while she mentioned that.

"In fact aunt, you might know his uncle very well. Almost everybody who lives in this town I guess, knows him."

"Whom are you talking about?" she asked.

"Shri Raj Singh Thakur"

I leaned forward to touch her feet, one of the old Indian customs foisted upon us by the society. But she stepped back in a very grotesque manner, turned around and said, "I will get water for you" and left.

"She did not like me coming here; I think." I actually felt a bit embarrassed by her behavior.

"Please don't mind. Actually, she is not used to strangers very often at her home. She rather prefers to be reclusive. Once you spend time with her, she will welcome you the next time with all of her warmth. Please have a seat and as ensured, I'll get tea for you," she giggled and marched in the same direction as her aunt.

It was both who emerged together. Sawmya with two cups of tea, and her aunt with snacks.

"Please have the tea," cheered the aunt, "and the samosas too."

Her attitude had suddenly shifted to a warm one. Sawmya was quite correct, but I did not expect this to happen so early.

They sat with me on the sofa.

"So how is your uncle? Raj Singh Ji is a renowned man in this town. When he was admitted to the hospital, it was the leading news," she queried.

"He is fine now, only that he has been adjured by doctors to rest for a while," I replied.

Later, she asked about me, what I was studying, how long I was going to stay here. I felt that I was being interviewed as if I had come to ask her daughter for marriage.

Suddenly, I deported into flashback. I was sitting in front of Anjana's father that day in his drawing room similarly, having a sip of tea and bites of samosa. Anjana was sent outside by him. "Listen young man, let us get it straight. I understand that both of you like each other," he began.

"Like? I love her madly, damn you!" I screamed inside my head. "I also know that these infatuations, which youth culminate now a days are like the seasons of a year that keeps on alternating. What I am going to say might disgust you, but it is the truth.

I have raised my daughter with utmost love and ardor. I don't want her to marry someone who is himself unsure of his own parentage. And to be more candid, I have already selected the bridegroom for her. He is the son of my fellow, Major Jaswant Singh. His name is Ranveer, an investment banker settled in Canada. You know what kind of family he belongs to? A chivalrous one."

I wondered what was his intention of furnishing the details to me as they were the last ones, I would have given damn for.

"You may not agree with me today, son. But may be twenty or thirty years later, when you'll get in my position of father to a *to be married daughter*, your notion for her groom shall be no offbeat."

I wanted to say to him, *that shall never happen.* If years later, my daughter comes to me with the proposal of getting married to someone she loves, that would be the only thing imperative to me rather than any stupid family background.

"You are correct sir! You are very correct! I came here to ask for your daughter's hand. Instead, you made me realize what a fool I had been all throughout my life. I believed that the only thing cardinal for two people in order to live happily ever after was true love. But today, I have cracked the books that there is more to this qualmish institution called 'Marriage.'

Anyways, thanks for the snacks. I think let Anjana herself adjudge what does she want. She is an adult after all," I said and left. As I was leaving I met her eyes, which were wet.

"I will wait for your reply Anjana."

I got her reply in that mail.

Sawmya aroused me from my past by her warm touch. "You seem to be lost again in your daydreams."

Yes, I did so in the bus too!

"So how is the tea, any better than the one at the restaurant?" "Not better, it is one of the best I ever had in my life," I said instantly in an ingratiating manner, having woken up from my trance.

"Oh cummon! You should be a little realistic in your compliments."

That's a nature common to all women, I believe.

First, they'll force you to compliment them like a foolhardy; and once you start to get overboard, they'll make you feel like a jerk.

When we were finished with the savory round of snacks, her aunt got up with the exhausted cups and plates.

"I will start preparations for the dinner. Sawmi, why don't you show Ajay your room till then?"

"Yes sure! Why not!"

She took me to her room upstairs. It did not appear to be of a grown up girl. There were a lot of soft toys stuffed in a large bucket, perhaps her entire collection of childhood. There were three different posters of Hannah Montana pasted in her room.

In the midst of a wall facing her study desk was a large photo frame displaying a picture of a smart looking couple with a little girl. "These are your parents and you, right?" I asked her.

"Yes, this picture was taken when I was probably three years old as aunt told me. That was a year before they met with the accident." Her tone became gloomy in the last sentence.

I continued to cheer her up, "You looked very beauteous in your childhood too, and so were your parents."

"Thanks, but my aunt says that my mother was far too charming in real life than in the photograph."

I instantly cut her down, "And you have truly inherited her charm in *your real life as well*."

She giggled over that comment. "Thanks for the flattering. So are you single or committed?"

I was suddenly taken aback by her inquisition, which came out of nowhere. "Well, I had been..." I embarked with the intention of telling her about the mess up I had recently undergone in my life, but then one thing was clear. My story with Anjana had come to a full stop. She was getting married to someone else. There was no hope of things reverting back to normal. So it was not a decent idea in drumming about it. "... had been looking for someone to be committed with. And I think I have found one finally, in this town. She makes very nice tea."

I do not know when I landed up with almost proffering her. When I realized it, I felt very asinine. But she did not seem to take it seriously. In fact, she laughed over it, "That's too much of flattering for the day. You must save some for tomorrow too." I wanted to tell her that it was not whimsical what I really began to feel about her; when her aunt called her "Sawmi, can you please come to the kitchen and help me out?"

"I will catch up with you soon; you can sit down for a while."

She left the room, but left behind her fragrance.

'Am I really falling for her?' I interrogated myself in my head. I had loved Anjana with all the fidelity in my heart, never philandered with any other girl, always dreamed of a glorious future with her. However, her acquiescing to her father's wish had shattered me. I always believed that she could have displayed pretty more resistance if she loved me the way I loved her. But maybe her love for me was not as assiduous as mine for her. My past again screened in front of my eyes. *Sawmya was correct, I was a daydreamer!*

After I received that mail from Anjana, I secluded myself from the rest of the world. And it seemed that it would be the end of days for me had I not received that call from Kabir, which made me get out of my hermit. Perhaps, I was destined to meet Sawmya that night at the bus stand.

Perhaps, I was destined to meet her again at the hospital. She was so elegant, attractive, and full of life. She may not be Anjana, but she was the kind of girl I wanted to spend my life with. *'Am I really falling for her or fooling myself in love again.'* Whatever it was, I had to give myself another chance.

We finished our dinner around quarter to nine. It was her aunt who asserted that I finish early and leave for my place as early as possible, due to fear of the witch who as per the belief was aggressive during the night. It was already dark by then. "You should hurry up. It is getting late and your house is far from here. Your uncle might also be getting worried of you," she sounded anxious.

Though narrowly, I had no belief in the witch story, I did not want to show any coarseness to her postulates either. I thanked them for the splendiferous dinner and left with my uncle's driver Mahindra toward home.

The drive on the way back was not serene. Our car gridlocked in the midst of the highway. Mahindra got out of the car and moved to the front. He came back and told that there was a large nail stuck in the front tire, which made it go flat. While he was doing the exercise of changing it, I came out of the car and seized a view of the highway. There was something outlandish about it. I went for a walk on the road, as it was deserted and it would have taken another ten minutes for the car to restart, as Mahindra forecasted.

The night stood among an ocean of darkness freckled only by the fewest of stars.

I would have walked for about two-hundred meters when I heard the crunching of footsteps behind me. I stopped and turned around. I could see nobody. Instinctively, my eyes went towards the car. Though I am not too sure, but I think that *I perceived a silhouette near it.* That shadow, what it seemed to me, was standing very near to Mahindra who was busy changing the tire and completely unaware of anything else. I advanced back toward the car at a much faster pace with my eyes fixed on it.

I am not clear till now, whether it was a male or a female figure that I saw. Whether it was the story about the imaginary witch that deluded me or was there really someone? Whoever or instead, whatever was there, did not show any sign of movement at all.

And then, it suddenly vanished out of the blue, or should I say in the dark!

I am still querying when and where did that thing dissipated, while writing this diary. On approaching the car, I asked Mahindra if he noticed anybody. He denied, but my query was plain enough to put wrinkles on his forehead. "Sir, please quickly get into the car. It is not wise to stay in such desolate places for long. Already, there are much back-fence talks in the town."

Once we entered the town, I noticed that the streets were completely barren. The shops were closed and public transport was on a stand still. There was not even a single person I could see almost for half of the distance, despite the time being just around nine pm. Then, there were quite a few people, scattered, perhaps the agnostics in the witch like me.

He dropped me in front of the main gate of the mansion. I walked toward the door and rang the bell. While I was waiting for the door to get open, *I heard the footsteps again!*

They belonged to Ram veer who came to open the door.

On quizzing, I was informed that uncle was busy doing some official work, regarding business documents along with his lawyer and does not want to be interfered. As for me, it was a long and tiring day; feeling very sleepy while writing my notes.

CHAPTER 5

TOWN HALL

Ajay's Diary –
November 1, 2010–3 pm

I am writing this diary after an abstinence of two days. A lot has changed during this short period. The catastrophe that has occurred is uncompensatable. I did not have the courage to pick up a pen and put it on paper, but I must resume now. It began as a routine day; I was having my breakfast with uncle.

"Kabir told me that you had gone to visit someone's house yesterday. That's all fine son, but you should be forethoughtful of whom you are making friends with in this town, as you are new here. You don't know the people around here. For them, you are just a rich man's nephew, and it is patent to everyone that as I have no family of my own, you are the legatee of my estate. People may try to artifice you in for their own egoistic reasons."

Somehow, I did not like his assertion even though all he had in his mind, was concern for me. I wondered how come he had learned all specifics of my whereabouts the previous day. I realized later that both Kabir and Mahindra were unwavering toward him. They would not lie to him in any event, despite the fact that I convinced Kabir to frame an apt story. I was a bit miffed with him, though I acknowledge his ardor to uncle.

"With all due respect, uncle, I met her incidentally in the bus. I did not narrate my profile or my relationship with you, to her at that time." *I partially lied.* "So there is no need to worry."

"I know Ajay that you are an insightful man, but you should be guarded. There are a few secrets about our family you need to know. And you will know them when the time comes."

"What secrets?"

"You will know them when the time comes," he repeated and left.

He left me dazzled, surmising of the secrets he just mentioned. My entire life had been a question mark. Who was the woman for whom my father left us? Where is he now? Is he alive or dead? Why did uncle lead an isolated life and kept me away from him?

Anjana's father was perhaps correct. *I was not sure of my own parentage.*

I too left with a puzzled mind.

I arrived at the restaurant, but could not find Sawmya. I sat on the same table we engaged the day earlier and waited for her. When nearly twenty minutes passed, I took out my phone to call her; instead I received the same from her.

"Hi, it's me! I am so sorry for not acquainting you earlier, but I shall not be able to come today. Here, near the town hall, something scandalous is happening!"

"What is happening? Are you alright?"

"I am alright dear, thanks for asking that," she tittered and then continued in a serious note, "a group of people have arrested a woman alleged to be a witch. Among them, there are priests of the Kali temple, which is the oldest and most visited temple of the town. The fact is that they are bolstered by almost all residents of the town, who now firmly believe that there is really a witch behind the murders. They have taken her to the town hall."

"It is so stupefying! How can everybody believe in a brainless story told by one man?"

"So you have not heard the news?"

"What news?"

"*Manohar is dead!* His body was found in the same manner as the previous ones in his house today morning. Also, the woman who has been captured is his wife, Savitri. People suspect that she is the witch who has been haunting the town for past several months."

"My God! That is so obnoxiously ridiculous! What on earth can make the people accredit so? And what more tragic can happen to Savitri? First, her husband has been killed and now, she has been branded a witch and implicated in his murder!"

"Ok, now I have got to go. I am trying to talk to one of these priests."

"Be careful, they may not like anybody catechizing their misdeed. I am coming, I will be there as soon as possible." I cut down the call immediately, not waiting for her reply. I was afraid if she tries to be gallant and argue with those people, it may hurt their sentiments, leading to untoward re- percussions. Although, I knew by now that she was obstinate enough to be held back.

'*Never argue with an angry mob, you can be their next victim.*' I read it somewhere.

It took me twenty minutes by car to reach near the town hall. A huge mob thronged outside of it. The noise produced by them was deafening. I could not make out from where to make entry into it to find Sawmya.

While I was wondering on my plan, I got a message on my cell phone. It was from her.

'Hey, do not try to enter the crowd if you have reached. Wait for me at the local bus stop nearby.'

I turned my eyes all around and noticed a small bus stop roughly two-hundred meters to my north. It was forsaken. There was neither any bus nor any passenger waiting for one.

I reached there. After around ten minutes, Sawmya appeared panting. "Glad, you have come! I managed to talk to one of the junior priests."

I intervened, "Just relax for a while. I cannot hear you clearly. Let us just sit inside the tea shop." I pointed toward a small tea stall. It also was vacated. Even the shop owner seemed to have gone to be a witness of the madness that was going on. We sat there alone on two chairs.

She continued, "I hardly managed to get out of the mob, which is growing stronger every few minutes to have a look at the so-branded witch. I have talked to Raheyshyam, a junior priest. I asked him what made them believe that Savitri is a witch and do they have any evidence of so? He told me sarcastically that she indeed is the witch, as Manohar was the only person who had seen the witch and was found murdered in his house that was locked from inside. Moreover, they will not directly take any action against her.

She will be kept seized inside a room with her hands and legs tied till she undergoes a trial to prove whether she is actually a witch or not."

"Trial! What kind of trial?"

"In the past, many women across the globe alleged to be witches have undergone trials. The result of almost all of them was fixed. *They all were conclusively proved to be witches and later burned, hanged or buried alive.* Haven't you heard of the infamous *Salem's trial*? I believe as a student of Arts, History should be in your curriculum."

"Salem's trial? Sorry, but I have never heard of it."

In January 1692, in Salem's village in Massachusetts, a nine-year-old girl Betty Parris and eleven-year-old girl Abigail Williams, who were the daughter and niece, respectively, of Samuel Parris, the minister of Salem village, began having fits, including eruptions of bawl and anamorphosis.

A local doctor, William Griggs, was summoned to diagnose and treat their ailments but could not find any. Instead, he suspected their condition to be of *bewitchment*. Soon other young girls in the community began to exhibit similar symptoms. In the late February, arrest warrants were issued for three women. Parris' Caribbean slave, Tituba, a homeless beggar Sarah Good, and a poor and elderly Sarah Osborn—whom the girls accused of bewitching them.

Though Good and Osborn denied their guilt, Tituba confessed that she had done witchcraft on the girls and was following the devil's order. Not only that she claimed that there were other witches besides her in the village. She might have done so, so that her acting as an informer might result in lighter action against her.

And that was not the end. The hysteria further spread across the village and beyond Salem into the rest of Massachusetts, a number of others were accused.

Like Tituba, several accused 'witches' confessed and named still others, and the trials soon began to overwhelm the local justice system. On May 1692, the newly appointed governor of Massachusetts, William Phips, ordered the establishment of a special Court of Oyer (to hear) and Terminer (to decide) on witchcraft.

The court handed down its first conviction in June, against a woman, Bridget Bishop. The place she was hanged is still infamous as *Gallows Hill* in Salem town. Five more people were hanged then in July, five in August, and eight more in September. Seven other died in jail and one was pelted with stones to death.

Other than the deceased ones, 150 other people, including women, men, and even children, were accused of witchcraft over several months. And, then it ended one day, when the court finally realized that there was no circumstantial evidence behind their conviction.

On January 1697, the Massachusetts General Court declared a day of fasting for the tragedy of the Salem witch trials. The court later regretted their act of injustice. However, the damage that was done to the community was beyond repair.

"That was so harrowing! But who will conduct the trial on Savitri? The priests?"

"No. The priests would not do it themselves. They have summoned a so called *Witch Doctor*. His name is Madhav Singh. He is around ninety years old and is alleged to have a vast experience in *witch-hunting*. He has proved many accusations against women suspected to be witches, guess what? True. He stays in a nearby village. So, it would not take long for him to arrive. In fact, he could be here anytime now."

I was astounded by her talent of compiling facts so quickly. She was superlative in her profession which had not yet kicked off.

"But how did you manage to get into the middle of the crowd and collect the inside story? I could not even dare to step into that."

"I told them that I am fiancée of Ajay Singh Thakur, the nephew of Raj Singh Thakur. Everybody here in this town knows and honors your uncle." *It was a straight lie though a beautiful one.* "And, I have tipped nicely the priest I congressed the info from."

"What are the police doing in all this matter?"

"They tried to stop it, but were simply outnumbered by the mob. The priests have warned them not to intervene. They said that the police have been unable to do anything to stop the murders, and now it is their culpability to do so in their own way."

"Then, is nothing going to forfend the poor women from dying?"

"No, the SP here, Rajesh Singh has been informed about this in the district headquarter. They might soon send a larger force."

Her phone blinked. She read the message, and then said, "It is from Radheyshyam. *The witch doctor has arrived.* The trial shall begin very soon. In this trial, few civilian men will be allowed as jury to validate it based on the chief priest's preference." She ceased for a while, and then continued, *"I request you to go inside and be a part of the jury."*

"Pardon me Sawmya, but I cannot watch the brutality that might possibly happen inside and why shall he allow me to be one?"

"Please do it for me. As a journalist I need a first-hand account of all that happens inside the four walls. I have already buzzed my channel people. They are sending cameramen and want me to get on the job straight away. And do not worry about admission. Radheyshyam shall arrange for it if he is interested in bigger tips."

I would have never done that, if it was not for her.

Half an hour later, I was standing inside the town hall. There was a large group of priests, most of them in past fifties. In the center was an elderly man seated in a different saffron wardrobe. He was the chief priest of the temple. Sri Sri Swami Madhusudan was his name, Sawmya told. He had smoky gray hairs and nebulous eyes. Though little frail, due to age, he still had a robust appearance. For the majority of the town people, he was a holy spirit, who spoke the word of god. *Our country is infected with so many of them.* Everyone has their own territory, of which they are the undisputed gods.

Surprisingly, the people I found invited as the jury were all reasonable men. One of them was an eminent jeweler who was well known to my uncle. Another was my teacher who taught me during my school days. Then, there were a few others I was unfamiliar with.

Fifteen minutes later entered even a more elderly man. His appearance was more of a *devil himself* rather than a *devil hunter*. Everything from his turban to his shoes was in black color. Even his eyelids were lined with black mascara and on top of that, he had anointed black nail polish. He bowed to the Swami Madhusudan and sat down beside him.

Swami Madhusudan got up from his seat and announced, "I welcome Madhav Singh Ji. As you all know, he has been a very renowned witch doctor since decades. He has brilliantly followed the footsteps of his father, the late Uddhav Singh Ji. Nearly, a hundred years ago, our town, which was a village then, was in the grip of a demonic witch who ate her husband and father. However, Uddhav Singh Ji came to the rescue and cataloged her in time before she could do more damage. Everybody knows the story what happened to that witch."

He was politically incorrect. I was completely birdbrained of what he was referring to.

"The witch has tormented our holy land several times since then, but has been taken care of each time. And now, years later, she has returned to this town in the form of late Manohar's wife. She has killed our men and ravaged the peace of this town. We are petrified to send our children outside to play, as we are not sure if they will return or not. Our occupations and businesses have come to a standstill, as we all are gripped in fear. This witch has not only killed few men, but also has smashed the very soul of our town. And today, Madhav Singh Ji has arrived to our rescue, as his father did once. Now, I am well aware that if we go around and execute this witch, based just on our beliefs, then you, the residents of this town may question tomorrow *that what was the evidence that she was a witch?* Hence, Madhav Singh Ji shall prove to us that she indeed is, *the chudaail.*" He turned toward his disciples and ordered, "Bring that witch here."

Five minutes later, they appeared, dragging a woman by her hair. Her condition was very pathetic.

She had severe bruises on her face and neck, which indicated that she was brutally beaten. Her handcuffs and leg cuffs were released, and she was shoved in front of the 'witch doctor.'

Madhav Singh, while seated bent down, caught her by her hairs and pulled her towards him.

While looking straight in her eyes, he interrogated loudly, "Tell me witch, where have you come from? And why did you kill all the innocent men?"

She was trying hard to speak; it looked as if her jaw had been dislocated, due to the thrashing.

She begged with folded hands. "Please release me Sahib. I am innocent, why are you doing this to me..." her plea was cut down by a thundering slap from Madhav Singh.

"Enough you witch, do not try to fool us! You already conned your husband who could not recognize you all these years. And when he did so, you killed him too! There is only one option in front of you, to confess that you are a witch. It will save our cherished time. We shall release you from this rotten body of yours without causing much pain. If you don't do it, then we shall put you to a death that you will never think of rebirth on this planet again."

She again tried to open her mouth with effort, "I do not know what you are talking about Sahib, please let me go. I have little children at home who are alone. They must be hungry..."

Another slap almost made her unconscious.

Madhav Singh got up from his seat and spoke, "Since the witch is not confessing herself, it is time to conduct a test, which shall prove that she definitely, *is the one*." He signaled to his subordinate who took out a bottle from his bag. It was almost a two liter bottle filled with some golden colored liquid.

Madhav Singh continued, "This is one of the simplest tests. As you all know that cow's urine is considered to be a holy drink in our religion. It is even accepted by modern medical science to have tremendous healing properties. Crores of Hindus use it regularly all across the country and even abroad. Therefore, for any pious Hindu woman it should not be a great deal to consume it. But for a demon, it is impossible to do so. Here is it, if she can devour a liter of it without vomiting, then we shall go to another test. But if she cannot do it, then tonight Jaisinghpur shall see history repeat itself again after a hundred years. She will be chastised as you desire on charges of witchcraft and murder. Do you all agree?"

"Yes! Yes! Yes!" chanted all the priests together.

Savitri was hardly aware of what was happening and what he said. She appeared to have been half fainted. Madhav Singh took the bottle and grasped her with her hairs again. He opened the cap and stuck the bottle to her mouth. Savitri first gulped it instinctively in hope of water, as she appeared to be severely dehydrated.

I sighed somewhat in hope that she also might be consuming that so called "holy drink" regularly like those crores of Hindus according to that madman. So, it should not be a great task for her. But, as soon as her stomach realized what had been put into her for the first time, she vomited it instantly in bulk.

"*Witch! Witch! Witch!* " Madhav Singh started to chant and was joined by all other priests. The chanting became louder and louder. There she lay wondering what had happened. She did not even receive a fair chance of being elucidated clearly of what she was being subjected to.

"Well, since now it is evidently established that this woman is a witch, now is the time to decide how to get rid of her. She has to be punished for the crime of murders of innocent people. But whatever is to be done, it should be over before it gets dark. As once it gets dark, we shall not be able to empower her."

Few of them shouted "*burn her!*," few shouted "*hang her!*," and others "*cut her head off!*."

As for me, it was getting too much intoxicated to withstand the lunacy.

I was developing an extreme dread and hatred for myself for being a witness to the crime.

When everyone's attention was on declaring the punishment, I swiftly moved back and walked out of the hall.

Sawmya was standing outside beside other people, waiting for the decision taken inside. "What happened inside? Is Savitri alright?" she asked me nervously.

"Somebody has to do quickly something, otherwise they will kill her. They have proved in their own way very quickly that she is a witch. And now they are planning how to murder her."

As soon as I finished my words, it was as if god had listened to me. There were a dozen police vehicles rushing toward us. Extra force had been called from the district headquarters. From the two main police vans nearly fifty policemen emerged, fully armed! They looked as if there were loaded for a battle. They were led by Rajesh Singh.

Rajesh Singh was an atypical looking police officer. His almost fifty-four-inch chest, banging his khaki shirt spoke of the fact that he had probably spent his entire life on a bench doing presses. He, along with his flamboyant mustache, reminded me of the actor Surya as *Singam* in a Tamil film of the same name.

As the policemen entered, there was havoc among the priests. They all gathered and blocked the way that led to Savitri.

"You fool! You are making a huge mistake! If this witch is unleashed she will not spare this town. Even you and your entire force cannot stop her. This is a golden opportunity to kill her and save our lives," Swami Madhusudan screamed at Rajesh Singh.

Rajesh Singh replied sternly, "We will take care of her if that happens, Swami Ji. As for now, tell your beloved disciples to get off, otherwise tonight we will be forced to welcome you and all of them as our royal guests, behind the bars. According to the order, issued by the 'Child and Women Welfare Minister,' Savitri and her children will be given complete police protection until she is rehabilitated in some other place. Also, if any of your people even tries to get within hundred feet of her then you will be sentenced to a minimum of six years in jail, I guarantee you," he announced boldly.

He took out his revolver and rubbed it with his handkerchief. Then, he said to a junior priest who was blocking his path,"Do you know one thing about a bullet, guru ji? It does not need a trial to judge whether a person is dead or alive."

I must say that though it appeared like a film dialogue, it worked very well. The priest got away instantly and so did everybody else.

He walked straight up to Savitri and pulled her up gently. Other policemen came forward and barricaded her. Swami Madhusudan understood that there was no use of creating trouble with the police, as they were armed and too many. Moreover, Rajesh Singh had come with a firm mind. He would not hesitate to open fire in the town hall. The police left with Savitri and left those people who had come prepared to murder an innocent woman, in anguish. We too left afterwards, to our respective homes.

CHAPTER 6

ADVERSITY STRIKES ME, AGAIN!

Ajay's Diary (continued)

The next morning, I was in deep sleep when a phone call by Sawmya woke me up. "Hi, I want to meet you urgently. Can you come right now?"

"What happened?" I asked while still half asleep.

"Madhav Singh has been murdered overnight!"

"What! How did it happen?"

"I will tell you once we meet. I have just talked to Radheyshyam. He has made some spookish revelations about the incident."

Forty minutes later, I was sitting in the restaurant in front of her. She repeated what Radheyshyam narrated to her.

Radheyshyam's Narration

When the police left along with Savitri, all of us were in despair. Swami Ji turned toward Madhav Singh and said, "Madhav Singh Ji, I know that what has happened here is calamitous. We let the witch escape from our hands. But these asinine policemen shall realize their erratum soon. When she turns into her original form tonight, they'll run to us begging for mercy. I think that we should not be disappointed. You should stay here with us tonight in the temple. May be tomorrow you esteemed services are required again; this time, by these scoundrels themselves."

"I agree Swami Ji, it is better to have some patience. Now, since the identity of the witch is revealed she will not remain quiescent for long and shall soon manifest her true colors. We will make sure that she meets her true fate."

Having said this, they returned to the temple. Everyone went to their respective places to sleep.

I had been sleeping for around two hours when I heard the screams. They came from the guest house. I lunged toward the guest house along with my other fellows. Soon, we realized that the screams belonged to none other than Madhav Singh. We hurried toward his room. Before we could reach there, we heard the thumping of gate, followed by a shattering sound.

On arrival at his room, we saw that the front door was thrashed into pieces. On entering inside we saw the body of Madhav Singh lying flat on the floor. It was disfigured in the same manner as the earlier ones. There lay a piece of broken glass, firmly grasped in his right hand. His left hand's forefinger was cut and was still oozing, indicating that it had been just a few seconds after the stab was made. It appeared as if he only had cut his finger, so that he could draw or write something. I looked all around, but could not make out anything. Later, when we lifted his body up to shift it on the bed, *we saw it*. It was smeared on the floor below where his body lay. We could not understand it. But when Swami Ji entered the room and saw it, he collapsed.

"What was it?"

"It was written in blood- *Not Savitri, it is Maya herself. She is back.*"

"Who is Maya?" I interrupted her narration.

He replied that he had heard fables about her when he was a child.

"Madam, I have been born and brought up in this town. When I was a small kid, my mother would forewarn me on not finishing my food properly. She would say *'If you do not eat your food, then Maya would come and pick you up. She would take you to her place and eat you.'* When I grew up I had forgotten about all those fables. When I joined the temple a year ago, I heard the story of Maya from a senior priest. He told me briefly that nearly hundred years ago, there was a young woman here in Jaisinghpur who used to teach poor children for free.

Later, it was discovered that she was actually a witch. She killed her husband and father, who were the first to unearth the truth about her. She was arrested and subjected to a trial by the head priest of the Kali temple. The trial was executed by a young witch doctor, Uddhav Singh.

She was proved to be a witch beyond doubt and killed for her crimes. *Her name was Maya.*

Everyone is babbling in the temple that Maya has returned from her grave and it is she, who is taking revenge on the town. She baited Madhav Singh, the son of Uddhav Singh, to come to Jaisinghpur, so she could kill him easily."

I asked her, "Are you convinced of this florid witch story?"

"Look, It is not about being convinced or not. I am a journalist and must go by the facts. Whether actually a witch exists or not is a hypothesis. The murders happening here are concrete. And there is someone behind them. To reach him or her, we have to go by the numbers. And there is one bottom line.

Manohar had seen an alleged witch that night. Madhav Singh was killed last night and he also mentioned about that woman who was killed a hundred years ago allegedly to be a witch. So, even if there is a real witch or not, someone is trying to create the ignis fetus of one. And till now he or she has vanquished admirably."

"So what is your plan now? What do you intend?" I asked her.

"Nothing. I am just waiting for police inquest and maybe the things shall get more apparent. As of now, I am free. What's your curriculum for the day?"

"Nothing special, maybe you can take break from this inquisition of yours and spend some time in exploring the beauty of this place. There is a very nice waterfall just outside this town, if you are interested. *After all, you are my 'declared' fiancée.* You ought to obey me." I brick bated her.

She laughed, "I hope you did not mind that. I just used that to get a way in."

"I did mind that and you have to pay back by accompanying me today."

"Ok. Even I have not been outside since coming here. But we shall be back before dark; otherwise my aunt shall deliver me a discourse again." We laughed together.

We spent the rest of the day enjoying the splendid scenic glossary. Jaisinghpur, though fleeting through dark times was still a sightly place. And the company of someone dazzling had just glorified its charm even more.

Though it was one of the most stupendous days of my life, the night that followed turned to be the cruelest one.

After dropping Sawmya to her home, I returned to the mansion.

By the time I reached the house, it was already ten in the night. I was bone-weary of the day and was heading straight to my room when I heard the cranking of a door. It came from upstairs where uncle lived. I went up. His room was not latched from inside, something very unusual of him. I pushed it open and went inside.

The lights were off, and it was very cold inside. I noticed that the main window was wide open. That was quite bizarre, as he never used to sleep with an open window. I went ahead and closed it. While I was clearing out of the room, I noticed that there was something unusual in the manner he slept on the bed.

It appeared as if he lay with his head toward the bed and feet twisted. Nervously, I switched on the lights and my horror came true. *Uncle had been murdered! He had been murdered in the same manner as all of them!*

Then I heard it! I heard the cry of a woman. I could not make out where it was coming from as there was nobody else in the room. It appeared as it came from outside. I opened the window that I shut moments earlier and gazed out.

At first, I could not believe my eyes; I blinked several times to confirm.

A woman in black dress was hanging upside down from one of the main branches of a tree. She was rolling back and forth, crying in a low tone. She probably didn't notice me yet. When she did, she howled loudly like a wolf. My heart flipped up to my awestruck mouth, I felt as if my soul had vacated my body. I stood there stunned. I wanted to escape, but my feet were frozen. I could not even blink further. She got down from the tree and stared at me, straight in my eyes. And then, she vanished! That was perhaps the moment when I languished, as I don't remember anything after that.

"Sir, are you alright?" I could recognize the voice. It was that of Kabir. When I opened my eyes I saw myself lying in my room. I was surrounded by Kabir and Rajesh Singh. "Are you alright sir?" He asked again. "Yes. I am fine. But how did I come here? And what you are doing here officer?" I had momentarily forgotten about the incident.

Rajesh Singh spoke, "Mr Ajay, your uncle has been murdered. His body was found in his bed. One of the servants found you lying unconscious on the floor of his room."

I recapitulated the incident. "Oh my god! How long have I been sleeping?"

"Sir that was last night. Your uncle's body has been sent for post-mortem," Kabir took over.

"Can you recall Ajay, what happened last night? You know it is just a part of our routine investigation," asked Rajesh Singh.

I told him that when I entered his room, I found his window open. On switching the lights on, I found his body in that manner on seeing which I fainted. I hid from him what I actually saw; as he would not have given credence to my ludicrous testimonial.

The inspector enquired about a few other things and then left. As for the funeral, we had to wait till the body was released after post-mortem.

I saw my cell phone. There were over fifty missed calls from Sawmya. I rang her up. She fired a series of questions on picking up the phone, "Where were you? Are you all right? Why didn't you pick up my phone? I was so worried. I heard about your uncle. How can this happen in your house?"

I was not sure which one to reply first. Instead the first thing that I said was, *"I saw her! It was her!"*

She was bewildered. "What are you speaking? What did you see?"

"I saw the witch. She is the one who murdered uncle." My voice trepidated when I mentioned about her.

"What are you saying? Are you in your senses? You only remarked the witch story to be a fancy one!"

"I know that. But what I saw is indubitable. I will tell you in detail once we meet."

"You need not bother to come this time. I will come to your place right away," she said and cut down the call.

Uncle's last rituals happened the next day. It was performed by Swami Madhusudan himself. At the time of his cremation, I came to realize what a great impact he had on the people. There was a huge crowd outside his mansion, even larger than the one I witnessed two days earlier outside the town hall.

Rahim also arrived from Mumbai. He was rooted in lamentation as his association with uncle was more enduring than anyone else present there.

After the obsequy was over, Swami Madhusudan came close to me and said, "Dear son, Raj Singh Ji was a great blessing to this town. He and his forefathers had nourished it with their own sweat and blood. I wish that you carry forward his emulation and rebuilt it. This town is going through a raucous phase. First, all those men, then Madhav Singh, and now your uncle!" He paused, "now the only hope lies with you. After all, you belong to the same Thakur bloodline. You must do something to stop it."

I wondered whether it was a genuine concern or fear of his own life, that he was galvanizing me.

After the ritual, people paid homage to uncle's photograph and started to leave. Rahim came to me, "Ajay baba, I know that it is time to stay here and take care of you. But another awful adversity has struck. My wife, whom I have not visited for almost a year has been suddenly paralyzed. I must immediately leave otherwise I will repent my negligence towards her throughout my life."

I said reflectively, "By asking so Rahim, you are embarrassing me. You have devoted not only the last year, but also your entire life for the service of our family. Words have not been conceived till now that can describe what you have done for us. Please leave immediately and do not worry about me."

The way he embraced me closely, I felt it was uncle himself. He whispered in my ears, "Take care of yourself baba, I shall be back soon."

After almost everyone had left, Kabir came close to me and said, "Sir, Raj Singh Ji's lawyer shall arrive tomorrow to discuss regarding the legacy of his assets. But there is something else I need to tell you. When Raj Singh Ji was discharged from the hospital, he handed me an envelope. As per his disposition, he wanted me to give it to you after his death, whenever that took place. He told me it was meant to be opened only by you."

He handed me a large envelope, which felt stuffy, as if it contained some document papers. When I was about to open it, Kabir intervened, "Sir, pardon me but as per his last wish, it should be done by you while alone. You can go to his study room for privacy."

I came to uncle's study room and locked it from inside. It was a sealed envelope.

I sat down in uncle's arm chair, wondering what could be there inside. Finally, after a series of clueless guesses, I opened it. There were a few letters pinned together. It did not appear to be any official document; it was handwritten by uncle. *In fact, it was a single letter, addressed to me.* I started reading it.

CHAPTER 7

MAYA

Raj Singh Thakur's Letter
Dear Ajay,

If you are reading this letter, it means that I am no longer in this world. I trust Kabir that before I die, he shall never give it to you. He is a sincere and loyal man, just as his father was. I am highlighting it because you are going to need his support in the days to come.

I could have told you myself directly what I want you to know. However, I know that having heard the entire truth shall make you feel shamefaced about our family. I understand that you have been through hard times in life. Your father abandoned you and your mother for another woman.

Your mother, my little sister; died with a cold heart. You have remained alone for the most of your life. I was very busy in my work that I could not raise you up personally. I did sent the money, but could not send my time along with it, son. I also know about your splitsville with Anjana. Yes, Rahim told me that! You withstood all the beastly circumstances that have come into your life, and I know that you are now mature enough to face the truth.

I don't know where to begin from. Ok, let me start from my ailment. All you know about it is that I had a cardiac arrest that landed me in hospital. But there is more to it. I saw someone that night, which shocked me to the core. When I woke up, I found myself in hospital.

That someone was Maya!

You must have heard her name by now, I believe. Yes Ajay, hard to accept but that's the truth. It might appear to you what a paradoxical man I am.

I saw her right in front of me. Why I survived that night? It is still an enigma to me. However, I know that it is not going to be for long. My end is near. Hence, I shall tell you about the ill events that happened here nearly hundred years ago. This story was told to me by my father while he was dying of a chronic illness.

A century ago, this town was a small village. That was the era of the landlords, era of kakistocracy. My grandfather, or to say, your great-grandfather, was the most powerful landlord of his time. His name was Baldev Singh Thakur. He was about fifty-six years old, a well-built man. He had three wives at the same time. Those were the days when the law of the land was made, manipulated, and broken by the rich and mighty. Although it was the period of British rule, but Jaisinghpur's landlords had made a deal with them that they would pay them annually a huge sum of money, lest they be left alone with their dictatorship. And the Britishers were satiated with that.

Baldev Singh Thakur was flagitious for his never ending lust of women. Despite having three wives he was an unfulfilled man. One day, he summoned his family astrologer who also was the head priest of the Kali temple at that time. His name was Anand Swami.

Baldev Singh admitted to him his intentions of marrying a fourth time. He appointed Anand Swami to find him a suitable bride as he had searched with his libidinous eyes in the entire village and could not find an apt one on his own. Anand Swami revisited him shortly after a couple of days with details of few blossoming gorgeous girls. Baldev Singh surveyed each of them, but as his expectancy had crossed limits, he shunned all of them.

Time passed, and then one bedeviled day, he saw a woman in front of the Kali temple. She was the most beautiful woman he had seen in his entire half-a-centurion life. He notified Anand Swami at once to seek for her and send his feeler to her house.

The priest visited Baldev Singh the very next day in a state of gloom.

"Thakur Sahib. I have enquired about that woman. Her name is Maya. She is the daughter of Omprakash, a school teacher. She herself is a teacher at home; teaches poor children for free, but..." the priest hesitated.

"But what?" Baldev Singh was madcap to know.

"Pardon me Thakur Sahib, she is already married and mother of a five-year-old girl."

Baldev Singh waited for a moment on hearing this, and then replied as if it was virtually trivial for him. "It does not matter at all Swami Ji. You go and tell her father that Baldev Singh Thakur likes his daughter and wants to marry her. Convince him to force his daughter to leave her husband and marry me. In return, I shall fill his mouth with wealth he cannot imagine in his seven births altogether."

Baldev Singh spoke as if he was not at all bothered about the fact that Maya was a married woman and a mother too. The dark cloud of lust had absolutely covered his senses.

"But Thakur Sahib, it shall not be that easy to brainwash him. I know him very well. He is a man of principles and a reverent teacher. He is not a kind of a person who will be interested in any money over the merriment of his daughter..."

Baldev Singh interrupted him in fury, "Swami Ji, that's your job to persuade him. You are the chief priest of this village. If he is such a decent man as you laud, then he should respect you and comply. I want that girl at any cost. *At any cost!* " He repeated to authenticate that he really meant what he said.

"Yes Thakur Sahib. I shall try my best." He got up, bowed, and left.

The same afternoon, he was in Omprakash's house.

"*Swami Ji, do you know what the hell you are discoursing?*" Omprakash was never before so much affronted in his life earlier. "If somebody else would have spoken this, I would have kicked his butt out of my house. But you are the head priest, considered to be the holiest man of this village. How can you ever come to me with such proposal? Do you not fear your gods while you utter such fraudulent words?"

"I fear my gods Omprakash, I fear my gods. But then, I fear Baldev Singh as well. My gods will not come on this earth to save me from him. Hence, you should too, fear him. I think you do not know him. If he wants something, he will get it anyhow, no matter what price he has to pay for it. And now he has set his 'eagle eyes' on your daughter. If you care about her, then do as I have told you. Make her divorce her husband and marry the Thakur. I will arrange for everything. Otherwise, he will not let you and your daughter leave in peace."

"Enough Swami Ji! I've contemplated you as a divine man till now. But it shall not be any longer that way, if you stay in my house for another minute. I solicit you to leave urgently. Otherwise, it would not look decent for the head priest of the Kali temple to be thrown by an ordinary school teacher out of his house."

Anand Swami got up instantly, "I am leaving Omprakash. But let me warn you again; you are committing the most dreadful mistake of your life. *The price of your inexorability not only you, but your daughter too shall pay dearly.* I came here as your well-wisher to save you from the apocalypse that has been bestowed upon you. But if you have decided to doom yourself, not even the gods can save you." Anand Swami left the house, frustrated.

Next day was the most caliginous in the history of Jaisinghpur. That day saw humanity being torn to pieces in broad daylight. Had that day not happened, there would not have been this dark hour that this place is going through. It began as a typical day. Everybody was rushing to their place of work. Omprakash was getting ready to go to school. A few blocks away, in her home Maya was busy preparing breakfast for her husband Mahesh, and getting her daughter Sharanya, ready for her first day in school. She had put on the bridal dress she wore on her marriage, as it was her sixth anniversary. She was extremely jubilant that day.

On the other hand, Baldev Singh was getting ready to carry out a heinous act that his upcoming generations shall regret until death.

While Omprakash was combing his hair after putting his new clothes on, he heard a knock on the main door. He wondered who could be there this early morning to visit him? As soon as he opened the door, he was shoved violently to the ground by a heavy hand. Then entered inside Tara, the most ferocious and favorite goon of Baldev Singh. He was accompanied by five others. One of them closed the door from inside.

"Who are you? And what do you want from me?" Omprakash cried, while recovering on his knees.

Tara said, "I will tell you Master Sahib who I am. I am Tara; the same Tara, who has committed twelve murders on just one signal of the Thakur. And today, I have come here to hike my tally if you do not do as he wishes."

"That shall never happen! Go and tell your Thakur that my daughter is not for sale. I do not fear anyone of you. I shall inform the police, they will put you rascals behind the bars."

On hearing it, everyone laughed. Tara said, "Although you are standing in front of your death Master Sahib, you talk funnily. Don't you know that the Thakur owns this village and the policemen begin their day after bowing to him? I think that today you will let me have the pleasure of increasing my score; although I have never done something like this that I have been told to do, *ever before.*"

As soon as he finished his words, the goons grabbed Omprakash. One of them clenched his head tightly and made him protrude out his tongue. Tara took out a knife from his pocket and marched toward him. *He was correct, he had never done something like this ever before.*

At Maya's home, Mahesh had left for work an hour earlier. Maya was returning back to her home after dropping Sharanya to school. As it was her first day at school, Sharanya cried a lot for her mother, insisting her to stay along. As that was not possible, Maya left with a heavy heart. Just when she was about to unlock her main door, she was seized from behind by two men. Before she could scream, another man stuffed a cloth in her mouth. A moment later, she was put in a carriage; her face was wrapped with a dark cloth so she could not see where she was being taken. Out of shock, she lost her consciousness.

When she came back to her senses, she found that she was lying on a large bed. There was a man standing at the door who bawled to someone outside the room. Soon, the room was filled with ten more, *five of which were the same who had visited Omprakash's house an hour earlier.*

Then, Baldev Singh entered the room just like a fox moves swiftly toward its prey. His eyes were red, as he did not sleep the night before. He had spent the entire night in anticipation of the moment that finally arrived. He sat in a large armchair beside the bed and lit up his cigar. Maya was too dismayed to utter anything.

"I never thought that it would end this way. The moment I saw you, I knew that I was going to spend sleepless nights until I acquire you. But I wanted to possess you respectfully as a wife. I sent Anand Swami to assure your father for the same. He instead assured the Swami that I am a scoundrel and a rascal.

Now tell me, what a scoundrel and a rascal should do? Should he sit quietly after being humiliated by an insignificant school teacher, or should he display what a scoundrel and a rascal he really is? *I chose the latter.*"

Maya was too frightened, "Please leave me Sahib! I regret if my father has disrespected you. Please let me go home. I shall tell him to plead mercy to you."

"Ha-ha!" He laughed aloud. "He will be pleading mercy to the devils in hell at this moment along with your ignoble husband and your daughter. There is no one left in your family my dear. Now, there is no one to come between you and me. Marry me and I will treat you like a queen."

On hearing this Maya was blown away. Those few words of Baldev Singh deserted her entire world in a moment.

Those few words meant that now there was no need to be afraid, as she had lost everything to get afraid of. She had lost her daughter, whom she had nurtured with lots of love. She had lost her husband who cared and loved her undisputedly. And she had lost her father who taught her all the moral values of life, to be honest, respect others and be a good person. And with that, she had lost her fear.

"You bastard! You coward! It is you who shall plead mercy to the devils!" Maya was furious. She charged toward Baldev Singh. She snagged his neck and tried to strangulate him but was soon pushed back by the goons. "Your soul will rot in hell! Not even the dogs will eat your fecal body, you scoundrel!" *And then, she spat on his face.*

Baldev Singh had reckoned the similar backlash from her, but her spitting on his face made him go mad as hell.

"You bitch, how dare you spit on me? Now I will show you what class you belong to. *You shall die the death of a whore and a witch, I promise you right now!* "

One of the goons nabbed Maya and pinned her down onto the bed. Baldev Singh came on top of her and did what he had been envisaging the entire night before. *He raped her.*

When he was done with his bestiality, he got away from the bed and said, "Now I shall fulfill the first part of my promise. As whore fucks with many men in her lifetime, I will arrange for all those many men for you in a single day." He turned toward his goons and said, "This is your bonus of the year, enjoy it well."

All the goons turn by turn did the ghastly act on Maya. The room that day was filled with her cries, her sighs, her pleas. But there was no mercy hovering in that room. All that one could listen was the laughter of the devils. The gods had perhaps closed their eyes, covered their ears, and shut their mouths; *or did the gods even exist? I sincerely doubt that.*

For Maya, that room was nothing less than hell. When all of them were done with the savagery, they dragged her by hair. Once outside, one of them kicked hard on her butt. She fell several feet apart. The beasts stood there laughing for few minutes and then left. Her body and soul had been crucified enough to get up and go anywhere. She laid there on the street for several minutes.

Finally, she composed herself and got up to her feet somehow. She had to go back to her house, she realized. What if the Thakur was lying? What if her family was still alive? She had to find it out herself. Though she felt extremely feeble, she had to get back to her house and find for herself. With a tint of hope, she got up and started to walk. The people on the streets were gazing at her strangely, as her clothes were torn and she was in a semi-naked condition. Moreover, she was bleeding from her vagina. She was leaving the stains of the misfeasance done on her chastity on the path she was walking.

After walking clueless for about half an hour, she got familiar with the streets. Now, she was close to her home.

She moved fast, not knowing that there was an even bigger horror waiting at her house. The street that led to her house was suffused with people. She realized that may be the Thakur meant what he said. There might be the corpses of his family lying on floor of his house and that is why the neighbors had turned up. She quickly hurdled her way through them.

The reciprocation of neighbors on seeing her should have been one of that of congeniality. Instead, everyone got away from her when she passed near them. They had a mixed expression of qualm and antipathy on their face. But Maya was more worried about the scene at her house rather than the neighbors at that moment.

On her arrival to her house, she did not have to enter inside to find the truth. The cold truth was out there, hanging from the ceiling in front of the doorstep. She wished that Thakur's men had killed her instead of her watching what she saw. She crumpled down on her knees.

The naked dead bodies of her father and husband were hanging upside down from the ceiling!

Their tongues were cut, eyeballs removed, throats slit, and abdomen burst wide open!

There was no sign of her daughter anywhere. She tried to cry hard, but her voice would not come out. Nobody came even close to her. There were constant murmurs among them.

One of the voices came from behind, "God have mercy on us. It cannot be the work of a human being. Only a demon could do that. There is she, the demon, the WITCH!!"

In her feeble consciousness, she could recognize that voice. It was of one of the goons of the Thakur who raped her minutes before.

She realized instantly what Baldev Singh meant.

You shall die the death of a whore and a witch, I promise you right now.

He had already fulfilled the first part of his promise, and now it was the turn of the second part.

It was all a set up that had just begun. The murmurs now became louder. She could not understand the sentences clearly, as there were so many of them. But she could understand one word common in them, *'The Witch.'*

People began to disperse due to panic, but the same voice roared again, "Do not run away brothers and sisters. If you run away now, the witch shall kill you later, as she has killed her own family. If you liberate her today, you have to live with fear every day. She will eat your children. It is time to teach her a lesson." At first, the people floundered but then they realized that he was right. They picked up stones and started to assail Maya. One of the stones hit her on the right temple and it started to bleed profusely.

Anand Swami arrived by then, encircled by his loyal followers at the scene at the right time. "What is happening here? Why you all are gathered here?" He looked up toward the dead bodies and burlesqued as if he was unaware of the situation. *"Good lord! Good lord! What calamity has occurred here? Who has done this awful act?"*

Everybody unanimously said, "It is the Witch! It is the Witch!" Now no longer her name was Maya. She was *the Witch* for the people.

Swami Ji looked at Maya and bethinked his words *'The price of your inexorability not only you, but your daughter too shall pay dearly.'*

Maya was indeed paying the price of her father's words dearly.

Swami Ji continued his iterated words. "Leave aside this poor woman. You cannot punish her as a witch until it is proved conclusively. Nobody gives you the right to you to kill her, simply based on arraignment."

"Then what should we do Swami Ji? If we leave her then she will kill us all?" came another rehearsed question.

"Leave this job to us. The learned ones will decide if she is a witch or not. I know of a young, but famous witch doctor in a nearby by village, Uddhav Singh. He will be summoned at once. This woman will undergo a fair trial. If during the trial, she is proved to be a witch then she will not be exempted at all. She will be executed in front of the entire village. Until then, have faith in your Swami."

CHAPTER 8

BURN HER ALIVE!

Raj Singh Thakur's Letter (continued)

Maya was dragged by Tara and his men to the Kali temple located two kilometers away. In the course, the entire village had gathered to see 'the Witch.' Maya could hear their voices amidst the gruesome pain. "Look at her, the Witch!"

"I always knew there was something green eyed about her. That is why she used to teach children for free. She might be drinking their blood too, who knows!"

She heard the voice of a mother telling her child, "Look Guddu, *that is a witch*. She ate her family. If you don't eat food properly, *she will eat you too*."

"Swami Ji is such a nice man. He is risking all his reputation to give a fair trial to this bloody witch, though she does not deserve one."

"Swami Ji is making a dreaded mistake by keeping this witch alive. She should have been killed immediately."

Once Maya was brought to the temple, she was tied to a pillar. Anand Swami appointed few men to watch her. *Those were the same men who raped Maya sometime back.*

He broadcasted to the villagers who amassed in front of the temple in large number.

"I am glad that all of you have rightfully abided by. You have confided in me and I shall not abort you. This woman standing here in front of you shall be punished rightfully if found guilty, of being a witch. However, if found innocent, then none shall harm her. She will be emigrated to another village. That is my responsibility. Now, Uddhav Singh is expected to arrive here in an hour; hence I shall request all of you to be patient till then. Once he appears, we shall begin the proceedings under his injunction."

Uddhav Singh arrived an hour later, as forecasted.

"Free her from the ropes," he ordered. This startled the people a bit, considering that she might charge at them once free. "Don't worry. Till I am standing on my two feet, this witch if she is; shall not even glance at you."

The men released her from the ropes. Once there was no support, Maya fell straight to the ground, having bled so much.

"Now, shall I begin the trial if you allow, Swami Ji?"

Anand Swami raised his hand, both as an attestation and sanctification.

"We shall give a fair chance to this witch to confute that she is one. She has to undergo three tests for the same. If she fails in any two of the three, then it shall be entrenched without any further doubt that she is a witch.

This is her first test. It is said that a witch can float in water. It is time to test it today for ourselves."

Maya was taken to the temple well. Her hands were clenched together and tied to a rope. She was bulldozed into the well. It was nearly fifty-feet deep with scarcely any water. Maya fell straight on her back. She felt that her spine had been broken into several pieces. She just missed her head, which struck the floor of the well after her back had taken the majority of impact. Their intention was clear from that act.

They had planned to kill her during the trials itself!

If she died, they would declare that the poor woman was innocent, but their job of getting her out of their way would be done anyway.

If she survived, she would be labeled as a witch and eventually be killed later. Uddhav Singh and Swami's men gathered at the mouth of the well and screamed, *"She did not drown! She did not drown! She floats! She floats!"*

There was a wave of panic among the villagers. On sensing it, Uddhav Singh exclaimed, "Do not worry. There are still two more tests left to go. Take her out." He ordered the men. It appeared as if they were pulling a corpse out of the well. At once, the men they thought that she was done away with. But, on noticing her breathing, they were startled. They picked her and carried her up to the main premise of the temple again.

"This bitch would not die soon," they murmured among themselves.

"My dear fellows, now is the time for the second test. It is said that a witch can turn her feet backward. Our man will try to twist her feet. If he can do it fluently, she again fails in the test."

Maya saw with her rapidly drooping eyelids the silhouette of a man walking toward her. *It was Tara.* He grabbed both of her legs in his arms and twisted them in succession. As he was muscular enough, it was not effortful for him to twist her feet. She screamed in agony.

Anand Swami turned towards the crowd, "My dear brothers and sisters, it has been proved beyond any doubt that this woman is a witch. She has killed her father and husband. Her daughter is missing as well. She might have eaten her too and thrown her remains somewhere. Before announcing her punishment, I ask you; the damn witch, to admit in front of everybody your true identity. Tell the truth and may be we shall consider of giving you an easier death. *If you don't, you shall be burned alive in* the *center of the village.*"

Throughout all the atrocities being performed on her, Maya had not spoken a word. Despite the life-threatening torture committed on her, she did not plead mercy. The people among whom she was born and lived, did not even gave her a chance to describe what happened to her. Nobody was keen to listen to her side of the story.

And now, those people were silent, rapt in attention when she was given a chance to declare that she was a Witch. Was she going to admit that? Was she going to admit that forced lie?

Maya got up partially on her knees. She looked around. She could see that the entire village had gathered to see her in that poignant state. There was more crowd than used to gather at the annual village fair.

There were people sitting on trees just to have a glance at her. There were people with children on their shoulders who did not understand what a witch meant. There were those goons who had molested her on orders of Baldev Singh.

There was Anand Swami whom she worshipped as a saint since she was a little girl, and who today planned and executed the entire drama. He was standing like a Messiah, savior of the village. She spoke, but she was not frail; she neither cried nor did she beg for mercy. Instead, she was furious.

"Today, you have hoarded your filthy souls to see a how a woman appears who has been brutally raped! You have congregated here to show your children the witch, who has killed her family members and ate her daughter! Neither did you show any sympathy while I was lurching on my way back to my house after being raped by Thakur and these bastards, who are standing with their heads high and chests expanded; nor did you let me mourn for my family's pitiless murders. Instead, you are interested to know who I am?

I am a WITCH! Yes, I am a witch. I have arrived from hell to kill you all. You motherfuckers think that you shall get rid of me by killing this mortal body? You are making the biggest mistake of your life. I shall return and not spare anyone of you. These children who are sitting on your shoulders and looking at me with fun in their eyes, shall understand the true meaning of a witch. They will fear for their lives when they grow up. Your coming generations shall shiver on hearing my name. **I, MAYA, THE WITCH**, curse you all. You will soon regret the day you were born on this land."

On hearing this, there was extreme panic among the villagers. They were frightened to the core.

Anand Swami came forward as their savior again.

"Did you all listen to what she said? She has admitted that she is the bloody witch. But do not fear. Nothing what she has uttered, shall ever be true. Instead, it is she who shall regret that she was ever born on this land."

He ordered his men, "Take this bitch to the gallows."

They dragged her to the back of the temple where already a gallow had been constructed for her. But it was not meant for hanging her. Instead, Anand Swami had a different plan for her.

He announced again to the people "In our custom, we burn the body after death. But to kill first and then burn her, would be a mild punishment. This witch who has disturbed the peace of our society needs a graver death. *She deserves no easier death than being burned alive.*"

Everybody started to chant, *"Burn her alive! Burn her alive!"*

One of the goons pulled her up on the gallow and tied her to a pole, especially erected for that purpose.

Then, another brought a large container and emptied it over her. It was kerosene!

She was entirely drenched with the every drop of it.

Anand Swami spoke again, "I am glad to announce that this witch shall be served with amercement by none other than the honorable lord of this village, Baldev Singh Thakur!"

There was a huge applause at the announcement.

Baldev Singh egressed like a jackal from the pack of his favorite goons. He took over the firelight from Tara and climbed up the steps that led to Maya.

Standing in front of her, he looked in her eyes and said in a low note. "Now, do you realize? This is the price to be paid to disobey Baldev Singh. Your dead father would have understood it well while watching from hell."

Maya, who still had a bit of fight left in her replied, "Kill me fast you motherfucker. Kill me fast! Otherwise, I will pull the testicles out of your body and feed them to the dogs on street!"

Baldev Singh was taken aback by her reply. "You whore! You bitch! Nobody talks to me like that! Nobody!"

He lit her body with the firelight. As there was an enormous quantity of kerosene on her body, it almost exploded into flames. The ignition was so fierce that Baldev Singh fell several feet apart from the gallow on the ground.

The loud flames were strong enough to have killed Maya in a matter of seconds.

It was the month of December, cold December. Never ever before, had it rained in that month in Jaisinghpur. There was no sign of it when the trial had begun or even when Baldev Singh was marching toward her with the firelight.

But it rained that day!

It is said that almost at the same time, when Maya was lit with fire, there was a burst of cloud. It poured heavily at the place. The flames that had engulfed Maya suddenly extinguished. This created tremendous panic among the villagers. They began to evade.

"It is the Witch's job! She has contrived the rains! She will not leave anybody!"

Baldev Singh got up on his hurt knees. He was very scared both due to the explosion and now the sudden appearance of rains. He too ran away, fearing for his life.

In a few minutes, the rain stopped as instantly as it had begun.

Soon, everybody began to cluster again near the podium to look what happened to Maya.

The charred body of Maya was lying on the floor of the podium. Her bridal dress was blackened, due to the soot. Her hairs were burned out. There was no flesh left on her divine face. Her facial bones popped robustly out of her skin.

She did not move at all for a few minutes. Everyone assumed that she was dead. Anand Swami and his men moved unhurriedly toward her.

Suddenly there was a flicker of her fingers. And then her right hand moved.

"*She is still alive!! The witch is still alive!!*" someone from the crowd screamed.

Anand Swami was too cramped by now. The fear that the unheralded rains generated among the people had already ruined his show. Also, now her being alive till now had liquidated his reputation in front of the villagers.

He asked Uddhav Singh, "What shall we do? No human being could withstand the torture that we have subjected to her. How do we kill her? How do we kill her?"There was a clear sense of deep panic in his voice.

Uddhav Singh replied, himself not sure what to do, "Swami Ji, we have already tried the best option of killing her. Now, the only way left is to bury her. Once there is no air to breathe, I wonder what magic she will perform in there. After the burial, we must construct a hall around her grave and lock the door secured with mantras."

The goons went forward and pulled her near corpse like body to the back side of the temple and began to dig her grave. There she lay motionless with her eyes wide open, watching her deathbed being build.

Once it was ready, they picked her up and nudged her into it. As she was being buried alive inch by inch, her eyelids began to shut down. Finally, her soul left the body that sustained the physical and mental trauma, no human being had ever been subjected to.

Dear Ajay, this is what I had to share with you; the dark and ignominious history of our family. After the day when Maya was killed, the villagers became involved in their routine schedule. They realized later that actually Anand Swami and Uddhav Singh did not generate enough concrete evidence that Maya was a Witch; they just managed to convince everyone in the heat of that moment. *After all, it was a fabricated trial*. The goons who raped Maya also sung their misdeeds openly.

People became aware that she was nothing but a martyr that day. It was a trap set by Baldev Singh and executed by Anand Swami and Uddhav Singh to flaunt what the value of an ordinary person was under the 'Raj' of the Thakur. As they realized the truth, they became phobic of him. They understood that one who did not obey the Thakur shall meet the same fate, as Maya did.

That day, it was not just a woman who was raped and murdered. The soul of this place was too, raped and murdered. An innocent woman was killed as a Witch. She was not a Witch. But she was made to be one.

She was made a Witch by the society.

And now she has risen from her grave. She is back with revenge. She was right, now the children who were making fun of the so called witch at that time have realized what it meant.

People are shivering on the name of Maya. Soon they will regret that they were born in this town.

This is our past, our family history, our shame.

When I was told about it by my father, I at once conjectured that I will make every effort to wash the misdeeds that were done by my grandfather. And I tried my best.

I worked day and night to feather the broken wings of this place. I left the ancestral house at once, as I could not breathe the air that was filled with the screams of Maya.

I quit high school because I could not carry forward my studies on the money, which had been amassed by the murderer of humanity. I brought up on my own efforts prosperity to this place. And now, I see it getting incinerated day by day. What's more deplorable than the people getting killed is that they are being assassinated in their psyche every day.

A life led in the fear of death is worse than death itself. I know what happened with her is not justified. But what is happening now is not legitimized either.

If everything continues like this, people shall flee this town forever. This place will be forsaken and become another name like Bhangarh or countless other haunted places in the world.

In all circumstances, Maya should be stopped! She must be!

By now, the people who inflicted torture on her, the people who watched her murder as a piece of drama are already dead. This generation is not censurable for a crime committed hundred years ago. It does not deserve any retribution. I accord the obligation of stopping Maya upon you. That was my aim to summon you. I know that by doing so, I am nailing your life in jeopardy, but that's what you have got to do for me and for this town. Ajay, you also have the option to escape the town and salvage yourself. But if you are resolute by now and are ready to do it, please read further.

I know of a man who can help you. In fact, you know him very well too. His name is Shashank Arya. He is a Professor in Theological science, in your college. I read a book by him nearly two years ago, "*Occult Practices in Modern India–My experience with them.*" It had a marvelous description of witchcraft being practiced currently in India.

If there is someone, who can help you at this moment, it is he. I have mentioned below his address and phone number. Call him immediately before it is too late. This is the reason I called you here Ajay, to rescue the people from Maya's revenge. That's my last wish. And I know, you would fulfill it.

Yours Ever Loving Uncle,

Raj Singh.

CHAPTER 9

SHASHANK ARYA

Professor Arya's Audio Tapes
November 2, 2010

After returning from Jawahar Kala Kendra where I had given a guest talk on *"The Occult India – Then and Now,"* I straight away went under the shower. It had become my beloved place in the recent years, where I could tranquilize after a day's exacting itinerary. Sometimes I ponder whether my schedules are taxing or my years, which are fast racing toward fifty? It is hard to convince people during such lectures that occult practices like exorcism, witchcraft, voodoo, planchette, does exist in our country even today.

Many times people debate with me that whether the solution to them is literacy; as they believe that such practices mainly linger in the villages among the illiterates. However, I can tell from my experience that the majority of such beliefs are widely rampant in educated and prosperous societies as well.

I can recollect one of the incidents that happened in a very affluent area. First, one of the children from the locality went missing. Initially, it was believed to be a kidnapping case, as the child belonged to a rich business family. But as no phone call was received by the parents in the upcoming days, the mystery deepened. Police investigated the case thoroughly, but everything was in vain. And that was not an isolated incident. Just after a few days, another child from the same neighborhood went missing, and then another. There emerged a state of terror not only in the respective colony, but also in the entire city.

After pressure from the citizens and the media, the case was shifted to the CBI. The chief investigating officer of CBI soon noted an interesting clue. All of the people whose children got missing were common friends of a couple. The couple was childless, but very fond of the children in their vicinity. Also, the parents used to leave their children with them often, as they had an image of a loving and caring one. But the officer chose not to interrogate them, as it would alarm them. Once when the couple was out of their house for their work, the CBI team raided their house. They searched the entire house, but could not find any trace of the missing children. While they were examining their bedroom, they incidentally discovered a secret door that led to a basement. They followed the steps to the basement.

As they stepped down, they felt enormous cold. To their horror, they discovered that the basement had been converted to a large deep freezer. *And their laid bodies of the missing children, five in all.*

All bodies were cannulated in their forearms and appeared dead pallor. Apart from that, all of them were in a perfect shape. It seemed as if only their blood was withdrawn with the help of blood transfusion sets. Beside that, there was no sign of any external injury on their fragile torso.

The couple was eventually arrested. During the interrogation, they admitted that they believed in paganism. And as one of the rituals they used to drink blood to increase their lifespan. First, it was all well, as they were restricted to devour animal blood. They could easily and legally obtain it from the butcher house. But later, as they became soddened with it and wanted to improvise their quality of taste, *they did the abhorrent.*

They would invite children at their home, after convincing that they would give them a bag filled with toys and chocolates. However, they should come alone without notifying their parents because if they told their parents then the bag would disappear in the air. All of the children believed the couple. They had to. *They were all less than five years old!*

I was summoned by the police to investigate their statements. I spent hours with the couple in custody separately discussing their interest in paganism. They stated that they were followers of a society, which believed in several kinds of unorthodox practices.

It was believed that drinking fresh blood was the key in maintaining health and vigor. However, the couple admitted that the society only permitted to use animal blood. What misdeed they had done by killing the children to taste the human (and higher quality) blood was solely their own malfeasance and no one else was responsible for that. They also lamented that what they had done was detestable and shameful for their society. In their lust for human blood, they had committed the most sinful and gruesome act for which they deserved to be hanged. But their regret was too late. *The little ones they killed were not coming back.*

Professor Arya's Audio Tapes
November 10, 2010

If it had not been for the requisition from a student from my college; I probably would have never come here. I received his call about a week ago, but as I was involved in the case of Bangalore farmhouse murders, I told him that there was no option left for me but to appropriately finish the ongoing probe and then visit him. There was no other option left for him either, I guess.

Finally, I arrived today in Jaisinghpur, a small town, which had flashed the headlines of almost every newspaper in the country for the past couple of months. I was escorted by a lad named Kabir, who was the secretary of that student's deceased uncle.

On the way to the mansion, I acknowledged that there was a strange kind of placidity in the town. There were scantily any people visible on the streets, though I could remark a lot of peeping eyes through the half-open windows that I passed by.

Whatever was going in this town had ingrained their lives to such an extent that they had become skeptical to come out of their sheds even during daytime.

As the path was almost deserted, it took us just five minutes by car to cover seven kilometers to the mansion; something I could not even fancy back in Mumbai.

I was received cordially by him at his mansion. His name is Ajay.

"Good afternoon sir! You may not be familiar about me, but I am a sincere patron of your talks and lectures, like many others in the campus.

I always wanted to meet and introduce myself to you, but never envisioned that it would occur in a manner like this. Thanks for coming to Jaisinghpur."

The crisp dark circles underneath his eyes made it very clear that he had not slept fitly in the last few days.

"First of all, thanks for the recognition, though I am not much creditable of it. All I have done throughout my life is to chase my passion of unveiling the occult secrets of this world. And the lectures you mentioned are just a pageant of my passion. Now, coming to the matter I have been summoned for, can you be more specific how I may be of your help?

As far as I have read, there've occurred few murders in this town, and it is the burden of the police or some investigating agency to find the truth behind it," I said.

"Sir, if the truth was so luminous and comprehensible; I would not have bothered you for coming so far. But the police and the investigating agencies have failed to bust it. As you already are aware of the strange murders that have happened here, the accepted belief is that they have been committed by a witch, Maya. Maya was a pristine woman who was accused of being a witch and killed here nearly a century ago.

I am mortified to say that it was my own ancestor who was behind the act. Now, she is back with vengeance."

He handed me a bunch of pages. It was addressed to him, written by his uncle.

I took my time to go through it. Ajay remained dead silent while I was reading.

Once I was done, I spoke, "Ajay, you have baffled me my dear. At one instance, you declare that you are adherent to my work, and at another, you talk like all those people whose uneducated minds have generated all these nonsense concepts of ghosts, spirits, Satan, and witches.

If you sincerely follow me, then tell me when do I not disapprove of blind faith?

In my twenty years of research, I have never come across anything that has substantially corroborated the existence of supernatural.

All of my work is based on occult practices in the society with the remark that all they do is beget chaos in the society and should be aptly dealt with."

"Pardon me sir. My intention was not to upset you. Just like you, I too never believed in the existence of ghosts or spirits. Neither do I believe in them now. You are rightful sir; this place needs an effective police machinery and trust me it has one. However, they tried their best to hunt the criminals and failed to deliver.

When I came here a couple of days ago, I too chuckled upon the story of the witch. I never listened to the explication given by people about the witch, as I thought that they were mere villagers, illiterate, uneducated fools. On the night of my uncle's murder, I saw her. I saw the witch. But it could have been a delusion, hence I have not even mentioned about it to you.

But there is someone whom I fail to disbelieve.

My uncle, Raj Singh. He was the most reasonable man I had ever known. He surpassed all the cultural and social misbelieves. Sati, the social evil, was abolished in the times of the British itself; that's what misbelief is. But it still exists in remote areas of our country. I know you might be more aware of that than me, professor.

One of the places where it still was being carried out flauntingly was Jaisinghpur, until Raj Singh Thakur took a strong initiative to fight against it. He was opposed by lots of local people. Some people even attacked him in rage. He was stabbed ten times for his antimony. But it was for his benevolence that he survived.

As soon as he was out of the hospital, he contacted the state ministry and pressurized them to curb the evil practice as soon as possible. It was for his relentless efforts that 'sati' saw its way out of here.

Though he was very rich, he did not put all his wealth in locker to die along with. He dissipated more than half of it to open charitable schools and hospitals, so that the poor in his village do not lag behind in receiving elemental education and fundamental medical care.

In this letter, he clearly connoted how much abashed he was to learn that such an atrocity had been done by his own ancestor upon a helpless woman. He was so much contemptible of the event that took place years ago when he was not even born.

When such a man says to me that the same helpless woman has now returned from her grave to avenge herself, I do not know what to believe.

When such a man says to me that the reason for the people living here in fear is the result of the misdeed of our family, I do not know what to believe.

And when such a man, sir, asks me in his last wish to do something to stop the witch and save these people who had no role in the opprobrious crime, I do not know why I should not believe... that this place... *is haunted by a witch!*

A witch, that my family has contrived. A witch, to bar whom is now my responsibility. A witch, who has no right to take away the lives of the guiltless."

Ajay paused for a while. He was on the verge of breaking into tears, had he continued longer. I could figure out what encumbrance was upon him to prevent the calamitous murders. Like his uncle, he was deeply remorseful for the brutal assault that was done by his great-grandfather on Maya and her family.

"That's why sir, I need your help. Maybe not to stop a witch, if you do not believe in one; but lest to solve the mystery. To solve the mystery, whether there is one or not. And if not, then what's happening here and how to stop it?"

"Ajay, like you my intention too, is not to dishearten you. I understand what you are going through. One sincere request of mine is not to feel guilt-trip about what happened in the past. The only difference between you and others is that you are aware of your past, and hence the offence committed by your ancestors.

Other people hardly know about their ancestors. I don't even know the name of my great-grandfather, far from the fact whether he was a gentleman or a ficher.

Every man is responsible for the deeds done by him, not by someone else. If you do not take credit for the entire good deeds your uncle has done for this town, how can you hold yourself guilty for what your great-grandfather has sinned?

Coming to the matter, I still find it hard to believe that Maya, who was killed nearly a hundred years ago, has come back and is now avenging her murder.

Even if I could believe it, I find it hard to digest why it has happened after such a long era. What made her take such a long time to rise from the grave and do so?

The people she is killing, if the story is to be believed, are not the ones who raped her, and murdered her and her family. They are not the ones who branded her as a witch. The miscreants have already died many years ago, probably due to natural death or some accident, who knows? If anybody was to be avenged, it was them. Or Baldev Singh, who I believe might have died of either heart attack or say what, cancer?"

"It was during a hunt, Professor. Those days when big-game hunting was not prohibited, he was enslaved to the sport. But some mishap took place and he himself was hunted down by a tiger. I have heard of this story since childhood and used to feel bad for him. But, today I feel rejoiced on brooding over it."

I continued, "Ajay, if you insist so; I will try my best in solving this chiller. But it will not be a *witch-hunt*; it will be a hunt for the truth. The truth behind murders and the truth behind genesis of the witch story. From now on, you and I shall work to seek the very truth."

"You are not alone, Professor. I too wish to join you in your endeavor."

We turned our heads around. It was Sawmya, the girl about whom Ajay described me later.

"But Sawmya, it can be very dangerous. I, being the kin of the family, am already at the risk like uncle. And your association with me during this engagement can put your life at risk too," Ajay replied to her rhetorically.

Sawmya seemed to me a smart, intelligent person. I interrupted Ajay and spoke,

"And how do you think you can be of our aid?"

She replied, "Sir, I am a journalist and can..."

"Ok then..." I cut her off.

"You are welcome to help. I will tell you soon what you got to do."

If at all I was going to involve myself in the case, I would need people who could assist me chasing after cues. A journalist indeed, would be fitting for that.

"But sir, I do not want her to be in any awful situation because of me."

"Ajay, you need not worry about her. She appears to be a brave girl. And to be honest, we need more than just two of us in this exertion."

"Then count me in too sir," forward came Kabir.

"I have spent sleepless nights since the death of Raj Singh Ji. He was more than just an employer to me and my father. He had done more than my father himself could do for me. I cannot live peacefully until I find out who is behind his murder."

"Alright, then we are a team. And we shall operate as one," I announced. "I want everyone to be gathered at dinner, so that I can allocate what you've got to do."

As we later met at the dinner, I allotted them their respective assignments.

Sawmya's job was to dig out the past of Jaisinghpur since Maya's trial. She had to search for history of anything that occurred relevant to *witch-killings*.

Ajay was supposed to find the place where Maya's body was buried and make arrangements for exhumation!

Kabir's assignment was to extract the details of murders that took place not only in the recent days, but also of all of them who were killed, due to alleged witchcraft in the last century.

Each of their jobs was a tedious one and required few days. We had no option but to wait until some substantial evidence could be gathered.

As for me, I returned to my home to collect my notes, handbooks on witchcraft, and few other things.

There was a strong possibility that the *alleged witch* would strike again someone in the meantime. But, I had no choice. My aim was to methodically solve the riddle and not merely wait for it to unfurl on its own.

All we could do till then was to keep our fingers crossed.

Professor Arya's Audio Tapes
November 15, 2010

We all met after four days. I was glad that each one of them had finished their task quite dexterously. But there was a grim, the town had lost another life to the *'witch- attack.'* This time the victim was Raj Singh's driver, Mahindra.

The witnesses testified to the police that they saw Mahindra running in midnight hour in the midst of the colony where he lived, crying for help. Some people opened their windows to see what was happening. They described that he was very afraid. He was constantly turning behind as if he was being chased by someone. However, people could not make out whom he was running away from.

And then they saw her! They saw the witch behind him!

She was wearing a black dress; her eyes were red as hell.

A similar description was given by Ajay when he saw the woman that night hanging from a tree.

As per their description, she clamped him in his claws and crawled up the banyan tree, taking him along with her. They heard his screams thereafter followed by a few minutes of silence and then saw his body falling from the tree. There was no sign of the witch coming down. This event also made everybody assume that the big banyan tree is her home. She lives on that tree and during the night, comes down to haunt the village. The impact of the story was colossal; the entire colony where the banyan tree was situated has been godforsaken. People are afraid to return to their homes, as they fear that they might become the next victim of the witch.

Whoever is attacking the people has to be soon tracked down. There is no more time to fritter away.

We sat down in the living hall with each of our groundwork ready. Sawmya spoke first.

CHAPTER 10

REVELATIONS

Sawmya's Narration

I visited the Jaisinghpur Historical Library, and searched for newspapers of the period during which Maya and her family was slained. It is a barefaced fact that during those times, accusing a woman of witchcraft wasn't a sporadic event. Even the news of women killed on the altar of witchcraft was sparsely of any sensation to the people. That's the reason probably that it was toilsome to find such stories on the front pages or in the leading sections. Most of them were cornered in some middle or last pages. However, to my bewilderment, I could easily pin out the news of the Maya's trial that flashed on the front page of the newspaper. May be that was due to the level of high profile involvement into it.

Much of the information in this news is nothing ancillary than what has been shared by Ajay's uncle in his letter, except that it has an entirely altered frame of reference.

The newspaper recites it as the 'lion-hearted act' of Anand Swami and Uddhav Singh, whose judicious interventions saved the lives of the people from the *most dangerous witch* of all times, Maya.

Further, it also mentions that it was an archetype of one of the fairest witch trials ever conducted in the Indian history. Leaving all the bullshit aside, there is no reference to the Maya's daughter in that or any following newspapers. What happened to her is not known to anybody. She went missing from the very day and was not heard of, anytime later.

Professor spoke, "Not hard to guess that she was taken care of Baldev Singh's men. Her body might have been thrown in a river or buried somewhere in the forest."

Sawmya continued, "To explore all the witch-related incidents since then, appeared a mammoth task. But to my another consternation of the day, the librarian, an old gentleman, had arranged all such newspaper excerpts in a distinct section. When I enquired him the ratiocination for it, he replied that his mother too was accused of witchcraft and chastised for the same. Though not killed, she was expelled along with her children out of the nearby village. On coming to Jaisinghpur, she worked hard as a laborer.

In days to come, she suffered from tuberculosis, for which she visited the government hospital. By then, the news of her *witch-hoodness* had spread here too. The doctor disaccorded to treat her any further. She was also kicked out of her job later.

He has seen his mother dying every day, due to dearth of treatment. This gentleman worked his own way out of misery and educated himself, while also working as a laborer in the night.

He has helped a lot of woman accused of witchcraft in his lifetime by rehabilitating them and arranging for some kind of employment. It is thus evident that when he became caretaker of the library at a much later age, he searched for all such news excerpts and arrayed them in a discrete section.

In his words, 'If you wish to know about the most heinous acts of cruelty ever committed against humanity, you are standing at the right place. This land is witness to the most number of witch-killings in the Indian history.'

He later commented about the current scenario and said, 'It is very rejoicing to know that Maya, who was killed in the most disgustful manner has returned as a real witch again.

This place and its people need shock treatment repeatedly as a reminder of what ghastly act was done here by their ancestors on the land on which they are proudly standing.'"

"What did he meant by her returning as the real witch *again*?" questioned Ajay.

"This is not the first time that people are being murdered here in this manner. In fact, since a hundred years, it is the fourth time this is happening. Every thirty years or so similar events have taken place and people have been massacred in a series. Witnesses have claimed that all the murders were done by a witch. Description of *the Witch* in all of the eras was the same - a woman, her face partly covered with her long hairs, wearing the same black-bridal dress."

"Then, how did the murders cease in the respective eras? Did you find any answer to it?" asked Professor.

"I put up the same inquisition to the librarian. He replied that the witch would stop by herself when nearly *a majority of the population is wiped away!*

People have tried several times to kill her, but instead they met their own end. According to him, to every new generation in this village, Maya would fulfill her last promise *of making them live in fear and to regret the day they were born on this land*, true. This is just the outset. According to him, the detestable is yet to come. Till now people are hiding in their closed homes, with the great misapprehension that they are unassailable. Soon, a time shall come when the same homes will become their graveyard. There shall be no place to run or hide. She will come and kill anybody she will wish to. There is going to be total chaos, and the people shall have no other option but to pray for a quick death, at her hands."

I asked him whether there was any way to affray her. He went into an uncontrollable burst of laughter like a mad man. Once he recovered from it, he replied,

"Young lady, if you are outlining to combat her, better plan for your next life from now on. She is the most ferocious predator ever born on this planet. It will be shrewd to evade this place and run away. Soon, that option will also evaporate from your table."

Everyone was silent for a minute. Then, Professor broke the ice.

"Although, I am still far from being convinced that there is any real witch behind the murders, it is indeed difficult to explain that why similar killings have happened repeatedly at such a large interval of years. It does not appear to be the action of one person or one group just to sire terror. The librarian may be of some help to us. I believe that he knows more about the truth than anybody else. I will personally meet him tomorrow and request him to band with us. What about your drill, Ajay? Did you manage to complete the weird task I accorded to you?"

Ajay's Narration
"Yes Professor. It was initially a Gargantuan task to persuade Swami Madhusudan to take me to the Maya's grave, but he

was hooked when I told him that if we don't do something to stop her immediately, then he, being a potential threat, could become her next victim. I construed the task given to me to Rajesh Singh. He is quite a perceptive police officer who could discern what I meant and at a short notice, got orders issued for exhumation from the magistrate. He was also personally present with me during the procedure."

Swami took us to rear compound of Kali temple. There was a barn he led us to. It appeared as if it was not as ancient as the temple.

"This is where her grave lies," said Swami Madhusudan pointing towards the barn. "It was built later. It was constructed under the cover of holy mantras, so as to prevent the witch from rising up again."

On seeing the lock, it was quite apparent that it had not been unlatched since put in use. We waited for some time, until one of Swami's disciples got the keys from granary.

Swami Madhusudan said before opening the door, "The last time it was opened, was nearly thirty-four years ago. It was my guru ji who opened it. I was standing like this disciple in one of the corners."

"Why it was opened at all?"

"At that time, similar murders were taking place and everybody knew it was Maya, the witch, who was doing it. Our guru ji opened this door and performed yagnas to calm down her soul. But he failed like the previous ones. The witch killed him too after a few days of the yagna. That's why I am granting you to do whatever it takes to bring this calamity to an end."

I could see the fear of death hovering on his face very evidently. As the door opened, there came a gush of rotten air.

It was so much stinking in there, that for a minute I had a gray out. The hall had been inhabited with hundreds of spiders, which ran out immediately as if they too were terrified of *the entity* that was buried in there. The surface of the grave was embedded with several small trishuls, perhaps during the earlier yagnas in order to constrain Maya's spirit within it. Rajesh Singh ordered the workers to commence the procedure.

"Wait inspector! We are excavating the grave of Maya for the first time since she was buried here hundred years ago. You should understand that it is not going to be a childish exercise. The witch may strike us any moment, as she is aware of what we are going to do. This procedure must be done under the cover of sacred mantras," Swami Madhusudan declared.

"Do as you wish Swami Ji, but I do not have time to ravage," Rajesh Singh said callously.

Swami and his disciples sat outside the barn chanting some kind of mantras meant for protection from evil spirits. *I wondered whether any of the mantras would actually protect us, if she struck!*

The workers started their job. I must say that, as they were digging, my heart ran into tachycardia. After having heard so much about Maya, I was finally about to see her remains. It created a sense of extreme anxiety inside me. After two long hours of digging, one of them noticed something. He shouted, "I can see a hand!" I was outside the barn when I heard it.

I quickly went inside to have the first glimpse of her skeleton. Instead, I saw a well-preserved hand! A hand with intact skin, though there was hardly any flesh left underneath it! They explored further. The body had not decomposed completely. In fact, it was mummified. There were pieces of torn clothes still left over it. Those torn clothes told the story of the brutality done upon the anatomy, which once belonged to an alluring figure.

I could hear her screams in my mind, as if they were happening in real. The mewls appeared as that of the day when she was being molested by Thakur's men. And they were getting louder and louder. In fact, I was not only the one who heard it. *Everyone standing there could hear it too!*

"Oh good lord! The witch is here!" Swami Madhusudan went into panic. I realized how much tremulousness was there in his voice. Everybody was stunned in their place. Nobody moved or spoke a word. I could hear her weeps very clearly. It felt as if it was coming from somewhere distant.

"I think we have made a big mistake in exhuming her grave! She is chafed and shall not spared any of us!"

"Swami Ji, be quiet. Let me search where this bloody noise is coming from," Rajesh Singh said and took out his revolver. He was a fearless man who was not startled by any impression of the witch or whatsoever.

His subordinates followed him. "Officer, better do not go outside if you care for your life. The witch is too strong and dangerous for you and your men to handle. It is wise to stay here. I will recite the mantras that will protect us," said Swami Madhusudan.

Rajesh Singh turned toward him and replied, "Save yourself Swami Ji with your mantras if you can. I am better off with this." He pointed toward his gun. To be honest, I was damn scared at that moment. I could not decide whether to go out or to stay in. By the time I could decide, the officer had already left.

I just stood there, awestruck. While I was standing there, my eyes went on Maya's mummified body in the grave. I felt as if its eyes were staring at me.

I too could not help but to glance back at it. It appeared as if those shrunken eyes were moving to and fro. I felt that I was under a delusion. But, I was not. *The eyes were really moving!* I felt to run away from there, but then I saw a snail emerging between the eyelids. I gave a sigh of relief as it was the snail moving that gave the apparition of the dancing eyeballs.

By that time, the mewls ended. I wondered who was making it. Were those real witch sounds or our mass hysterical imagination or something else?

Rajesh Singh and his men returned in a few minutes. "Well Swami Ji, I could not find your witch. I think she ran away on hearing the clang of my metal." He said with a tint of risibility.

"Officer, do not take the matter lightly! The witch is browned off. She is demented because of what we have done today and will surely strike someone of us."

Then, he turned toward me and said absurdly. "Now, tell me what do you wish to achieve? I have allowed you to dig up her body. What the damn you want do with it?"

I replied, "Swami Ji, I want this body to be shifted to my hospital for examination."

"Examination! Are you out of your senses? What possible examination you want to do on this body, which hardly has any flesh remaining on it?"

"It's not the flesh; it's *the bones* I want to get examined."

"Bones! What on the earth you want to do?"

"It is beyond your discernment Swami Ji. I will let you know afterward. I just need to get the body shifted to hospital right now."

"Look you boy, I have allowed you thus far because you are Raj Singh's nephew and bloodline of the Thakur family that once ruled this land. But now, you are going too far when you wish to take away her body. The witch shall try to re-enter the body once it is out of the grave. And if once that happens, no one on the earth can save this place. She will become rhapsodical and unconstrained. Hence, I cannot allow you any further in this flumadiddle of yours."

I was going to reply when suddenly Rajesh Singh intervened, "Swami Ji, let him do as he wishes. May be we can acquire some clue about what's going on here in this village. Till now, we have failed to decipher anything about this mystery."

"What mystery, SP Sahib? What mystery? Don't you see what's going on here? That bloody witch is out yet again, thirsty for our souls. In the past too, she has brought calamity to this place. And if she repossesses her body, she will become more viperous than ever before."

"That we shall see when it happens. Till then, let the body be taken away. I have already got the orders issued of the possession of her body," he said so and without waiting for the Swami's response, signaled his men to extract the body out of the grave. Swami knew what Rajesh Singh was capable of doing; he had displayed it well a few days ago in the town hall. I indeed admire his will. He is a fierce officer who does not listens to anybody, except for himself. I think our country needs more of such policemen.

Swami murmured to himself, "Do not come begging to me when something terrible happens to you idiots" and left the scene. I could hear him chanting some kind of mantras, as he was leaving. It was fear of his own life that had startled him rather anything else.

Soon, we got the body transported to our hospital. After the drift was complete, Rajesh Singh told me, "Ajay, I have done whatever you asked me to do. I will also help you with anything you wish further, but do not disappoint me.

I am too not sure like Swami what you intend to do with this corpse; but whatever it is, *do it*. As in charge of the law and order of this place, I do not want to make people feel spineless. Till now, we have not been able to come any closer to the truth behind this case, now my only hope is you and the Professor.

Though I am a disbeliever in the supernatural, I must admit that what is happening here is no far from one. At my risk I have extracted the body and handed it over to you.

If at all anything happens, what the Swami has foretold; I shall not excuse myself for the blunder that I have possibly committed."

I ensured him that all that was being done was for the good, and the Swami's prediction shall be proved wrong. But sincerely speaking, sir, even I myself am not sure what will happen?

The noises that I heard back in the temple are still poising in my psyche. Who else's it could be other than the witch? And how did the body was still preserved in that state for a century?

"Ajay, do not exhaust yourself with too many assumptions and predictions. It is not surprising to me that the body's architecture was preserved. At times on burial, the fate of a body depends on many conditions, like the climate at that time, the nature of soil, manner in which death occurred, and the microbial flora of the grave.

So leave that fear of you aside. Now, coming to the pursuit, I have summoned my forensic friend from Delhi. She will be arriving here in a day or two, to perform the required tests on the body.

Just make sure that till then, the security at the hospital is perfect. Some miscreants like the Swami may try to retrieve the body back to the grave or destroy it out of panic."

That should not be a problem sir, as Rajesh Singh has himself arranged up the security at the mortuary, where the body has been kept. In his own words, *"Not even a fly can flutter in there without my approval."*

That is better, so Kabir what about you? Did you obtain any information about the linkups of the murders? I bet I had given you a much harder work.

Kabir's Narration

"Maybe sir. It might have been tougher concaving the past than the grave. But, the information that I have collected so far is astonishing. It appears that the murders that have taken place were not arbitrary. As Sawmya disclosed, these incidents have repeated themselves several times in the past, and there is a clear link between the people who were killed."

"What kind of link? What do you mean to say?"

"The majority of the people who were murdered in each of the era were the direct descendants of Baldev Singh's men, the same allegiant goons who carried out the heinous crime on Maya. It was impossible to gather information about each of them, due to non-availability of any records or any witnesses from the eras. However, I did manage to harbor some facts about a few of them."

The man who was the head of Thakur's goons was Tara. His death record is still handily obtainable in police archives. His murder was one of the most grisly of that time. It is noted in the records that Tara, along with his companions, was returning in late night from a nearby village.

They were crossing the anastomotic forest, known as the *'Kaala Jungle'* or *'Black Forest,'* when they saw a woman sitting with her head down in the midst of their path; covered in black satire. They asked her, who she was, and what was she doing in the middle of the forest? When the woman did not respond, Tara bared her head.

According to one of the goon, who survived that night, the woman was none other than Maya. He could not recollect anything more, as he fainted at the spot on seeing her. *Tara and two others were found the next day in a severely mutilated state, hanging naked from a tree upside down.*

It was similar to the manner in which Maya's father and husband were murdered. But it was more grody, due to the fact that all the viscera in their bodies was missing and never discovered as if some creature had eaten away every bit of it.

The goon who survived hanged himself the very next day. He left a small note in his pocket, "We have committed a heinous crime. She is back from hell and shall not leave anyone of us. I just want to die an easy death. God, please forgive me for my sins."

"What about Baldev Singh? Any information on that?"

It is a common knowledge that he died accidentally during a hunt. But there is more to this parable. That day, Baldev Singh went to hunt in the same *kaala jungle*, where Tara was killed a few days earlier.

As a usual protocol, he went well armed with an entire team of hunters and expert villagers. It is said that when after waiting for a few hours a tiger appeared to drink water at the nearby pond, Baldev Singh aimed at its head and shot from his favorite rifle. Baldev Singh was famous as an expert shooter. He never missed a target that he aimed for.

But that day he missed! The bullet hit the tiger in its leg, and it disappeared with a limp in the nearby bushes. Baldev Singh was very embittered on missing the shot. As he was aware that the tiger had indeed hurt its leg, and therefore now it was an easy prey, he ordered the rest of them not to follow him.

He went alone with his gun into the bushes, so that he could prove that he had hunted down a tiger without any body's aid. Moments later, they heard him screaming. They all rushed toward the bush and discovered Balder Singh in a severely wounded state. His abdomen was burst out. He was bleeding profusely.

There was also a doctor in their team, but the nature of the injury was way beyond his competency to deal with. Baldev Singh was rushed to the local hospital, where he was declared 'brought dead.'

The local police later went to the zone, where the accident took place and found to their surprise that the body of the tiger was lying just meters away from where Baldev Singh was found. The bullet that he and his men misinterpreted to have hit the leg, actually had struck its heart.

The tiger had died seconds later, after being shot. Moreover, on the post-mortem, it was found that claw prints found on the Thakur's body did not belong to the tiger or any other animal. But most shocking of all, *a piece of black cloth was found inside his intestines!*

Coming to Anand Swami and Uddhav Singh, the priest was found dead in the same temple well that was the part of Maya's trial and the witch doctor's body was discovered buried in a grave behind his house.

That was during 1916, when these events took place. Now coming to 1953, thirty-seven years later, a similar series of murders took place in Jaisinghpur. Overall, fifty-eight people were murdered in a matter of a few days. It is confirmed that thirty of them were kin of the goons.

Few of the witnesses stated that they had seen a woman in a black-bridal dress wandering alone in the streets at midnight around the houses of those who were killed. But nothing was proved conclusively.

Then happened, the most infamous murders in 1981, when seventy-nine people were killed again in succession of a few weeks. What was infamous about it was that people who thought that they were under threat by the witch escaped to distant places. Some of them went to nearby villages; some went to their relatives in town. But that was of no use. They managed to escape the village but could not escape their death.

That was the second generation penalized for the crime their ancestors had committed.

Now, it is the third generation.

If you believe the entire facts to be true, the town is paying for its deeds even today. And it seems, that it will continue to pay till the last man standing.

CHAPTER 11

IT'S LOVE, AGAIN!

Ajay's Diary
November 16, 2010–11 pm

It has been off late, since I have penned down anything in my diary since uncle's murder, but today, I feel to write once again. After meandering alone in the sea of melancholy, I can finally see the shore of a serene land.

I must continue from the moment, when we left Professor Arya with our revelations yesterday.

"Hmmm...," Professor muttered to himself and became silent for a few seconds.

"All the epiphanies that you guys have made has flustered my belief momentarily." He continued, "to find any other suitable annotation to it appears alien at the moment. However, it is still premature to arrive at any final conclusion. If that is the truth, and this town is definitely under the grip of a witch then we have got to put an end to it. If there is something else in the closet, we must debunk it. We cannot afford for the *alleged witch* to splash up with one more cold meat to her credit.

We ourselves have to go after her. Before that, I must share with you a few facts. If we are really considering the possibility of paranormal into it, my biggest question is what form of it are we dealing with? In the paranormal society, it is a colloquial that a person after death can manifest in several ways.

One of them is an orb, which is the most common manifestation. In the form of an orb, a spirit appears as a sphere, which is quite butterfingered of doing anything evident. Similarly, there are other forms, such as ectoplasm, which also has been described as a modest projection. In our case, I think we are dealing with an elemental form or a demon one, both of which are dangerous.

Another theory is that her spirit has possessed some body. Now, that is the reason why I asked Ajay to carry out the exhumation. It is evident that Maya's body was lying intact in the grave since it was buried.

Hence, if it is the spirit of Maya, which becomes agile every three decades or so, she needs to possess someone else's body, without which theoretically speaking it is impossible to make the physical appearances and further, perform the murders.

I shall also require information about the missing women during those events or in the present; someone whose body is possessed by Maya and is executing as the witch herself.

But whoever that is, she must have an abode where she lies dormant when not in a murderous frenzy. We need to predict it and start our search from there. I know what I am speaking is crazy; it is like trying to catch a lion in its own den! But that is better to do rather than just sitting like a sheep, waiting for the lion to attack suddenly from behind."

I spoke, "Sir, I can suggest you such a place, where we can look for her; where she might be vested."

"I hope you are not talking about that banyan tree, where Mahindra was killed. I have checked it out, there isn't anything over the tree," said Professor.

"No sir, it is the *black forest*, which has been mentioned today repeatedly. Thakur Baldev Singh was killed there. Even Tara and his men were murdered in that place. Recently, one of the victims, Narayan's body was too discovered near it. And to share with you my personal experience, once when I was returning from Sawmya's house, my car got stuck on the highway off it.

While I was waiting for it to be fixed by Mahindra, I noticed something odd in the air coming from that forest. It thought it was a phantom, when I noticed a dark figure moving toward him.

Seconds later, it was nowhere. Now, if may connect the strings together, it might have been the witch, who came from the black forest. Mahindra's murder few days later also tends to negate what I considered my delusion initially."

Professor said, "The black forest appears to be good lead Ajay, though of the little knowledge I have of it, it seems to be astronomical. Searching for her there would appear as firing an arrow in the dark."

Kabir replied to Professor, "Pardon me sir, but I too want to propose the black forest. One of our housekeepers, Ram veer is an expert about the black forest. Raj Singh Ji was very fond of trekking forests and mountains, and Ram veer has escorted him several times in the black forest as well. Once, he told me about an old house in the middle of the forest that he happened to come across. According to him, he did not dare to enter the house because of its murky appearance. He said that it was a perfect place for the witch to reside, and further added that if ever we intend to visit the house he would guide us to it."

Professor spoke, "Then, the black forest shall be the place where we begin our quest. However, we shall not go alone. There is someone else I need to hang around with us."

"Who?" Everyone asked.

"The librarian. I think he could be a valuable asset in our search. On meeting him tomorrow, I will convince him on coming with us. Kabir, I shall give you a list of items that we will need on our pursuit.

It shall be I, Ajay, Ram veer, and that librarian, if he agrees, who head for the black forest. Kabir, your engagement shall be to retinue my forensic friend who will arrive tomorrow and arrange for anything that she might need in her inquest. And as for you Sawmya, I think you better wait for us till we come back. The status quo in the forest may be unpropitious for you."

She sneered, "Sir, please do not exclude me from the expedition. Do you think that I cannot handle the forest as you can, just because I am a girl?"

"That's not the case Sawmya. Try to understand what Professor means. Moreover, you need not leave your aunt alone," I intervened.

"Well, if she judges that way, then I don't want to brunt her to stay back," said Professor.

"I too agree with you sir," then I turned toward her and continued,

"But, I have already lost all the people I ever loved in my life. I don't want to lose you too out there."

"But Ajay... I... I...," she perhaps wanted to tell me that she shall be unscathed in the forest, but was overwhelmed by my sudden outburst of love for her.

Both of us remained silent looking at each other. Sometimes you don't need a gallery of words to express emotions, they express themselves right away.

Professor spoke, "Well, it is for you to decide Sawmya. We will welcome whatever decision you take."

He continued, "As of now we must retire. We shall meet tomorrow at lunch and format our next plan of action then."

Everybody rose up and left the room. I whispered into Sawmya's ears. "Please come to my room. I need to talk to you."

Sawmya said, "I too want to talk" and followed me.

Once inside, she sat down on the sofa. I sat beside her. "Sawmya, I hope you were not irked by my words back there."

She just kept looking in my eyes elegantly without giving me any hint of what was going in her mind.

I continued, "But, what I spoke is the truth. And the truth is that, *I love you*. It happened the moment I saw you on the bus stand back in Delhi.

I have not slept a single night since that day without picturing you in my *fool's paradise*. I don't need your answer now. In fact, if the answer is no, just don't say it. You may not realize, but you have given a whole new essence to my life. I don't wish to sound comical, but if it was not for you, I would not have the courage to face this noxious situation at all.

It does not matter to me if you have someone already in your life. I will continue to love you, as it is necessary to sustain my vitals."

She chuckled at my last sentence. I recapitulated if it was stupid. *Perhaps, it was not.*

She replied, "If the reason that you do not want me to go to the forest is your love for me, my reason for going along with you is no different. And yes, I do already have someone in my life. He is there too, since I met him on that bus stand in Delhi."

Did I hear the right words or was I daydreaming again? I don't know. Neither did I care. I just leaned ahead, took her in my arms and kissed her. She too allowed herself to fall into me swimmingly. I felt the warmth of her breath for the first time apart than that of her hands that I had seasoned earlier.

She parted her lips from mine and said, "I love you too Ajay" and then we kissed again, and again like we had been waiting for each other since centuries. I didn't realize when we shifted our love to my bed. Very soon, I was on top of her, undressing her to installments. With each move, her angelic body was getting disinterred more and more till absoluteness.

Although, she had been on the forefront in all matters, she was quite submitful when it came to love making. As for me, I was just lost in her warmth to the fullness. It was all hypnotic. Being so close to her made me forget all the racking circumstances that I had gone through during the past few days.

Soon, we were out of our breaths. I lay beside her fondling her hairs. She said, "It is getting late. Aunt will be worrying. I should leave now, Ajay."

"No Sawmya, not tonight. I would not let you get away from me, especially this time. Already it's dark and it is not safe to go out there. I will call up your aunt and give her some valid reason for you staying here."

She moved closer to me. "Even I don't want to go. I will admit to her about us tomorrow, if she questions." She laid her head on my chest and soon we fell asleep together.

The next morning was one of the most airy and optimistic one. I had not slept so tranquilly since many weeks. I turned around to look for Sawmya, but she was not there. While I was wondering, she entered the room with a plate. It had two cups of tea.

"Good morning," she came to the bed. She kept the tea cups on one side and we kissed each other. She handed over to me one cup and took her's.

"Why did you take the trouble of making it yourself? You could have ordered any of the servants."

"Would you like to be pleased to taste your servant's hands first in the morning, or mine?" she said in a twitter-pated manner.

We kissed again. Then after taking a sip from the cup I said,

"You do make a very good tea, and I want to have it every morning when I get up in the bed. That's why I request you not to come to the forest. As far as my safety is concerned, it will be easy for me to worry about a single life rather than of both of us. So, I will be glad if you stay back with your aunt here."

"But Ajay, I do not want to leave you alone now since we have proposed each other. I want to face whatever may come together with you."

"We will face other difficulties and hardships of life together that may appear but not this one. And don't be cynical. I promise to you that I shall return safe and sound.

Once when this peril is finally over, I will visit your house officially to ask your aunt, her little niece's hand."

She embraced me tightly, "Oh Ajay! I pray to god it all happens the same way."

I too prayed to god for the first time in my mind for the same.

We gathered for an early lunch in the dining at 11.30 am, following which we shifted to the study.

Professor Arya spoke,

Professor's Narration

I have just returned after meeting the librarian. His name is Akbar.

I briefed him about our plan to investigate the 'witch mystery,' and asked him if he could help us in anyway. On listening to me he said contemptuously, "Why do you want to save the sinners? Let her kill all the bastards! The women of this land have suffered a great deal on false accusations of witchcraft. Now, when finally the people are facing a real witch, they are shivering! Let them dither, let them die! They deserve it! And I will give you a serious advice, gentleman. You are an outsider and need not risk your life in this matter. If you impede her in any way, she will not spare you too. And speaking of the house, that shall become your grave if you go in there. Recently, one of my servants happened to slip into the house.

He was returning from the nearby village, when he decided to take a short cut and entered the forest. On his way, he came across the house, where he made the foolish attempt to explore it. He saw something inside the house, which made him run away from there.

On returning, he told me that he saw *the witch* in there, and said that he was lucky to escape.

His body was found the next morning in his room in the same mutilated manner.

That house is the gateway to hell, if you believe my words. So better return back where you've come from. This place is heading toward perdition, let it be that way."

Once he was finished with his warnings, I said to him, "You speak of running away from this place, old man. Tell me where risk is not there. Life itself is the biggest risk we that kiss every day. I would've been glad if you could share with me something more about this matter but as of now, your revelation of the house is enough. You've cleared my doubts about going at all to the forest and that house. Thanks a lot for that."

After meeting him, one thing is evident; we are perhaps leading in the right direction. That house may unfold many mysteries. We will leave for it at the very first light tomorrow morning. "Kabir, did you arrange for the equipment that I listed?"

Before he could reply, one of the servants intervened. "I am sorry to disturb you sir, SP Sahib has arrived. He is sitting in the drawing room and wants to talk to you."

"Rajesh Singh? What business he might have at this moment?" I told him to send the officer inside.

Rajesh Singh entered inside the library, greeted one in all and sat down.

Ajay asked him, "So what's the news officer? Do you have any lead into the case?"

He rested back, took his time and said, "I do have one and I would like to thank you all for it."

"What do you mean by that?"

"Don't mind, but I am trying to do all that I can to solve this mystery. Even if that requires to spy someone. During the last few days, I had placed my men behind you guys. They were closely monitoring you since Professor's arrival here. And finally, when one of them told me of your plan of adventuring the forest, I have come to ask you, 'Hey! Do you fellas mind if I join you in this hunt of yours.'"

I spoke, "Officer if you wish to do so, we will be more than elated. To have someone like you, brave and daring in our quest, shall infuse a tremendous deal of mental strength into us."

"Thank you Professor, I am honored by your words. You guys shall be accompanied by me and my men. Whatever perils you may encounter over there, my men and I shall take care of it." Rajesh Singh stood, as if he was ready for a battle.

"Tomorrow morning officer, sharp at eight after breakfast," I told him.

"After breakfast!" He announced it loud in a dignified manner.

CHAPTER 12

BLACK FOREST

Ajay's Diary
November 17, 2010–10 pm

Next morning, we all were ready by eight. *Indeed, after breakfast!* Rajesh Singh introduced us to his constables; Raghu, Mohan, and Ramlal. I had already met them at the Kali temple during the exhumation.

"These are the best of my men. The witch shall not dare to come near you with them being around."

He was overconfident, *a good sign for us!*

Sawmya and Kabir were standing there. They too were pining to come with us. However, Kabir was entrusted by Professor Arya with another responsibility and Sawmya had held back, due to my reassurance to her.

We embraced each other for a minute. She said, "I wish I could join you. Now, I shall wait for you here."

I replied, "Don't worry, I will be back soon."

There was nothing more to be said; especially, in front of everybody.

We boarded our van and sat out for the black forest. We drove on the highway to the spot where I had seen the shadow that night. We parked our van beside the highway and took out all the imperative equipment.

"How long shall it take to reach there?" I asked Ram veer.

He replied, "It is almost fifteen kilometers from where we are standing, Sahib. But fifteen kilometers in this forest are consonant to fifty kilometers, as the terrain is difficult. It has rained well this season, so we must expect thick greenery hailing us on our way.

We also have to be aware that there are wild animals in the forest, which we may encounter, like tigers, bears, and wolfs. Hence, we have to be buttoned up while moving, not to attract any unnecessary visitors."

"One more thing," added Professor Arya. "If at all the witch stays here, then we must accept that we are right in her territory. She might try to attack us or harm us in some way or other. Therefore, we have to remain alert about any of her signs. If you see anything suspicious in this forest that you all don't understand, inform me at once. Also, remember, the witch might beguile us in any form, *so better be cautious than dead.*"

We carried the equipment in bags on our shoulders and barged into the forest.

We were led by Ram veer. He was our guide for the safari. He was followed by Rajesh Singh and his men, then Professor and I.

It was an oak brown forest. I wondered why it was termed '*black.*' It was certainly not due to the color of the tress or the bushes, perhaps it was after the color of pessimism that was so evident in there. The trees appeared as if they had been standing there since the creation of earth, staring down at us. The thick bushes in our way proved Ram veer's assumption to be correct. We had to frequently chop them off to clear our way. As we moved on, the foliage became thicker and lusher making it more difficult to walk. The forest had an unusual smell; though not obnoxious, it was not a pleasant one either.

It had been several hours of walking straight without a break. It was close to dusk. I was the first among them to halt, "I think we should rest, as I am too tired to walk any further."

Everyone stopped instantly as if waiting for an excuse. We sat down on the rocks.

"How far is the house Ram veer? It's been so much distance we have already covered as of now."

"We have traveled just around five kilometers Sahib, and still got a long way to go. I think we should lay off here for the night as soon it will become very dark and futile for us to go any further."

Everyone agreed with him. We set up our tents. Ram veer was correct. Just in few minutes it was dark. It was just six pm, but appeared as if it was midnight.

Ram veer brought some woods from nearby and arranged for a bonfire. Professor Arya initially suggested against it as to avoid attention of the wildlife and *may be of the witch*. But as it was getting very cold, he later dictated Ram veer to collect the woods.

We all sat near the bonfire relaxing our calves, which had taken a great deal of victimization for the day.

Rajesh Singh spoke, "So Professor, what do you think of it? Are you convinced of the existence of the witch or is there still any ambiguity in your mind?"

Professor Arya said solemnly,

"To begin with officer, I have been a part of several such situations, where it appeared initially grossly supernatural but later turned out to be something else. I have witnessed haunted places, possessions, devil worships, human sacrifices, and other such things and I can tell you that there was more to mass hysteria, delusions, and blind faith into a majority of them rather than anything else.

In this case, though evidences are mounting up one by one for existence of the supernatural, I sincerely hope that they all prove to be false.

The very concept of an entity of a *witch* has led to innumerable incidences of injustice to women.

Like Maya, many women have been tortured, raped, and murdered accused of witchcraft. And that is not the problem of the past. According to National Crime Bureau report, more than 1,700 women were killed in India just between 1991 and 2010.

To mention their latest report, just last year itself 117 women were killed in the name of witchhood. Hence, this stigma is still very fresh in today's times and not related to a century old or so.

Very recently, in Jharkhand, a mother and daughter were dragged by villagers to a nearby forest. Their throats were slit. They were accused of witchcraft on the account that the village children were getting sick. The mother was a widow and was living with her daughter alone. Hence, they were an easy victim of the mass hysteria that is yet far from getting over.

In another incidence, two women in their fifties were killed by three boys of their village. The father of one of the boys had died recently, and the fathers of two other boys were ill. On someone else's acquisition, the boys went to question the women. On their refusal to give any kind of justification to their questions, the boys got furiated. They first strangled and then slit their throats.

In 2001, the Jharkhand government passed the '**Dayan Pratha**' or the 'Prevention of witch practices' to stop the increasing atrocities against women. However, after more than a decade, witch-hunting in the state is still rampant. The fact speaks for itself.

While rape and murders of the women alleged to be witches have been a major evil, even other humiliating tortures on people accused of such, have been not been less than disgusting.

In July 2008, a woman along with her husband was forced out of their house. They both were accused of witchcraft, as the village livestock was getting sick. They were forced to eat human urine and excreta.

In Odisa, three people that included two women were paraded naked accused of witchcraft.

This night shall end soon, but then there is no end to the account of the atrocities which have happened in the past in our country and the world in the name of witch-hunting."

Mohan said, "Sir, I think that Maya is taking revenge for all the atrocities done in the name of witchhood. My mother has seen her cousin sister being murdered for being a witch.

In her words, what all is happening is justified. It is the outrage of all those innocent's cries that have never been heard. She says that Maya has been sent in this avatar of her as a witch straight from hell, as there is a shortage of occupants in there."

"That we shall see. As of now, it is getting late. We should better go to our tents and rest. We still got a long journey to cover tomorrow," Professor Arya said.

We all retired to our tents to sleep. But right in the woods, in the silent darkness, among the wild animals and with the lurking danger of a witch, sleep was far away from my eyes.

I laid on my mattress, epitomizing how my life had abruptly switched in just a few days. It seems like yesterday when I and Anjana were going so well together. I never expected that things would turn so sore between us. I was living in a false dream of a romantic and settled life with her.

My only aim in life was to make Anjana happy. Life as such was so enticing and full of buoyancy. And now, I was in a haunted forest, with my life at risk alongwith few men, I had not even met a few days earlier.

There was a strange kind of placidity in the forest. Or maybe it appeared to me strange, as it was the first time I was spending a night in the forest. There was no sound of mad crowd, cell phones, vehicles, machines, etc. All I could comprehend were chirps of the birds, dance of the leaves, and howls of wolves somewhere distant.

I could see light coming out of Professor Arya's tent. He too was tossing and turning in bed like me and was probably going through his notes in torch light. Rajesh Singh was quite undisqiuted. He seemed to be fast asleep. Though he had a tremendous burden on his shoulders placed by the higher authorities to resolve the murders, yet he had not entirely fallen to the belief in the witch as almost all of us probably had.

Finally, sleep hit me.

A few hours into my sleep, I suddenly started feeling very cold. In my dreams, I saw a shadow approaching me. As it was adventing toward me, I felt colder. Half slept, I covered myself with the blanket completely.

However, that did not give me any comfort from the cold.

Dead are cold! Dead are cold! The words ran through my mind.

I realized what the words meant.

The witch was approaching us, with the intention to kill! She was dead! And she was cold! It suddenly aroused me.

On awakening, I gave a sigh of relief. It was just a dream. But I still felt immensely cold. I looked outside. The light of Professor's tent was off. He had fallen asleep. Rajesh Singh had already succumbed to it earlier. The other constable's tents too were silent.

After rolling several times back and forth in the bed, I entered a partial sleep state.

During the rest of the night, I heard unusual sounds off and on, like crunching of twigs and snapping of branches. I assumed it to be just another kind of dream, and hence did not give any attention to it. Soon, I was dead asleep as well.

It was the outcry of Raghu in the morning that woke me up. In fact, it woke everybody up. I came out of my tent almost at the same time as others. He was standing in the midst of the tents.

"What happened man? Are you all right? Why did you shout?" Rajesh Singh yelled.

Raghu did not speak. He had an intonation on his face as if he was struck by lightning. He pointed his finger toward the ground. I stumbled on watching the horrific scene that lay below our ankles.

There were bones scattered all around us.

They looked like animal bones with shreds of flesh on them. It appeared as if it were left over from a fresh hunt.

A fresh and a mass hunt!

"What the fucking hell is this? Who in this damn world would do it?" screamed Rajesh Singh.

"It is a classic *witch-sign*, sir. It is forewarning from her that if we don't turn back then our fate shall be no different. I have seen similar sign earlier too. However, this is the first time when I am seeing such a heap of it. Seems like all the forest animals have been slaughtered," said Ram veer.

"Whatever it is, it is not a good omen. Even if all the animals have not been killed, the rest will be arriving here shortly, following the smell of fresh flesh. We have got to move quickly from here," Professor said.

We hurriedly repacked our gear and continued on our journey. It was still a long way to go. That incident made one thing clear. We were on the right track in search of the witch and not wasting our time there.

Kabir's Narration
November 18, 2010

I was waiting for Helena, the forensic friend of Professor Arya, for the past two hours at the town bus stand and she finally arrived.

"Hi! You must be Kabir. Shashank told me to expect you. Where is he?"

"He has gone on an expedition with few people in the nearby forest, Ma'am."

Professor told me not to mention to her about *the alleged witch-hunt*. He said that Helena was a much more rational person than him. In his own words,

"...and listen Kabir, don't mention to her about what we have assumed about the murders taking place here. Keep her distant from the local people or even the policemen till she completes her job. If she gets the idea that I have called her to examine the body believed to be of a witch, she will leave straightaway. She doesn't likes to get involved in anything she considers absurd. I have known her closely since college days. She even considers me the most imbecile man she has ever come across."

I continued "... an expedition to search for some old herbs that might be useful for treating the arthritis he is suffering from."

"Arthritis! Well, he never mentioned to me anything about that. So we are going to the hospital right?"

"Yes Ma'am. Please get in the car." I opened the door for her.

"Thank you," she sat on the back seat, "and if you like, you can address me just as Helena. Though I am a college mate of Shashank, I am not any Professor or so."

"Ok Helena, if you want it that way."

After a ten-minute drive, we reached the 'Jaisinghpur Seva Hospital.' The hospital was now turned into a fortress.

There were policemen guarding each of the entrances. At one of the gates, the disciples of the Swami were protesting.

They were demanding the body of Maya to be returned to the temple. According to them, Ajay and Rajesh Singh had fooled the Swami by possessing the body. They were assured that the once the investigation of the body was over, it would be returned. But, they were getting too appetent to wait. *"You fools, the witch will enter her body and kill the entire town."* I took Helena through the back entrance.

She enquired me about the protest. I told her that they were furiated about the death of some priest in the hospital and were demanding action again the doctors.

She remarked, "What's happening now days? *Everyone is against the doctors!"*

On reaching the mortuary, the attendant opened its door. As he already knew about her arrival, he took us straight to the deep freezer where Maya's body was kept. He slid the freezer out.

"I have kept everything ready for you, madam," he said in an ingratiating manner.

After inspecting it for a while Helena said, "So, that's the body I have got to examine. *Bone scan*, as Shashank mentioned. I wonder what he is up to. He never discloses to me anything till my work is complete. It has been his old penchant. So Kabir, are you going to tell me something or has he instructed you to be quiet and not to bias me?"

"Helena the truth is that... yes! he has instructed me to be quiet for whatever reason you may understand."

She laughed. "Ok then! I shall need my red luggage inside here. But be careful while it is being shifted. It contains my portable X-ray machine, that I have got issued from the institute where I work."

I myself went and together with the ward boys of the hospital, got her baggage shifted to the mortuary.

It took her another hour to assemble the equipment. Once ready, it looked as a standard X- ray machine. By my curiosity, I asked her,

"Pardon me Helena, but why did you take the trouble of transporting it when we already have an X-ray machine at the hospital?"

"It is a unique machine, Kabir. The routine X- ray machine that is used in hospital detects the activity of the osteophytes or simply speaking the live bone cells and projects the image. However, in a dead person, the osteophytes are already dead. This X- ray machine doesn't rely merely on the activity of the osteophytes; instead it can calculate the percentage of the dead osteophytes. And that's what is required to predict the age at the time of death. But it is just only a preliminary investigation, for more expert analysis, I need to shift the body to my center in Delhi."

"I am sorry Helena, due to reasons that I cannot furnish to you, that might not be possible. I mean, transporting the body out of this town. Can't you arrange for something down here?"

"There's an alternate way. For analysis, there is no need of the entire body. I need to take samples from this body and send it to my lab. With further tests, it will be possible to ascertain the exact time period this body belonged to, the exact age of it while death, the manner of death. As for facial profile, I need good quality cameras to take still photographs of her face. It is quite possible to generate the exact facial appearance of how she looked at the time of her death."

"That will be just great Helena. When you shall leave with the samples? Professor shall require the reports soon, I guess."

"I won't leave. My assistant shall arrive tomorrow morning and pick up the samples. It will undergo Radiocarbon dating, DNA profile study, and photographic analysis, the results of which shall be available to us in a day or two.

As for me, I shall like to spend some time in this quiet place. Back in there, I don't even have time to die. I needed a break since long. Moreover, I want to meet Shashank. I have not seen him for years together. He is quite an Argonaut," she simpered at herself.

"Ok Helena, I shall make your arrangement at the mansion. You are our guest," I said mixed with an element of joy and grim, for reasons I knew very well.

I wondered at that time how Professor, Ajay and others would be in that black wintry forest?

CHAPTER 13

HOUSE IN THE WOODS

Ajay's Diary
November 18, 2010–9 pm

After traveling for a few hours, we halted to eat something. While we were having our meals, a strange kind of noise erupted. It came from the trees.

"Now, what the hell is that?" asked Rajesh Singh, to nobody in particular.

"That is the sound of the monkeys. They usually make it whenever they see a predator coming; a predator like a lion or a tiger!" said Ram veer.

We all became wary at once. Rajesh Singh took out his pistol. The constables also aimed their rifles in the direction where the monkey's sound came from.

Whatever it was, it was moving toward us as evident by shaking of the trees and bushes. Also, it was big and huge enough as apparent by the tremendous agitation of anything that came in its path.

"Everyone, heads up! It is coming! Wait for my signal before firing!" Rajesh Singh dictated his subordinates when the last tree between it and us chattered.

It was a pack of tigers, four to five in all!

Everybody froze for a moment. I could see the right index finger of Rajesh Singh tensing. I wondered what

Rajesh Singh was waiting for as he had not fired yet. Then, I realized that the pack was not coming toward us! Instead, it was running somewhere else. But after whom? I could not see any game, which the tigers were hunting after.

They brushed past us and evanesced in the dark dense foliage.

The horror was over. Everyone gave a sigh of relief. We all sat down, drenched in the sudor of trepidation. I could still feel not only mine, but everyone else's heart pounding too.

"Close huh!" said I.

"Today is our propitious day that we escaped those predators. Otherwise, right in the jungle, in front of five of them, our bullets were of no match. They would have taken us down very easily," Rajesh Singh said.

"What happened, Professor? You don't feel relaxed! I can still see the frowns on your forehead," he remarked to Professor Arya, who still had a glare of dubiety in his two eyes.

"I am glad that we escaped being preyed upon. But, I am wondering what those carnivores were running away from?" said Professor.

This statement by him made everyone jump on their feet again. It was clear that the tigers were fleeing away from something, but we could not see any other animal or hunter behind them.

Then, we heard the cries! The same weeps that I heard back in the temple when the exhumation took place. Rajesh Singh and his men were also present there then, so they recognized the mewls as well.

"It is her! It is her! The witch! " said Mohan.

Rajesh Singh signaled them to aim toward the sound. Soon, it was coming from behind. Or maybe from the right! Or left! In fact, it appeared as if it was coming from all directions, or else the entire forest itself was weeping. We all cohered together. Was it was the witch, the tigers were running away from? Professor was dead on, we were standing right in her territory, *ready to be hunted!*

Soon the cries stopped. But, the palpitations of our hearts did not. We stood like a Siberian for a few more minutes, just looking for any sign of the witch who might appear from anywhere. There was an exceptional silence in the woods. *It was like the silence of the lambs, before the storm.*

However, there was no sign of the storm either. After around half an hour, Ram veer said.

"Sahib, we must set in motion now. The house is still far away. In this forest, it does not take long to get dark." He pointed to the sky, which was hardly now visible, shadowed by the tall egregious trees.

Amen to his words! *It had already begun to get dark.*

Days were like a fable in that monstrous forest. The name *Kaala jungle* or *Dark forest* was very appropriate for it. We tried to wrap the remaining distance in haste, so that we could reach the house before dark. Although, the possibility of such seemed far from legitimate. *After walking for another half an hour it was dark again!*

"It's just been a few hours since dawn; how the hell can it get dark so soon?" Rajesh Singh was frustrated.

"I think this forest is under the witch's spell, which is fond of darkness. Heard those cries? I wonder if we have not committed a mistake coming in here," said Ramlal.

"Shut the nonsense! We must focus upon our goal of coming here, not on any inept doctrines," Professor replied sternly.

We adjourned again and reset our tents. It was a long night and sleep was again a stranger, so we went into the usual confabulation as the night before.

I was damn enfeebled of the day, both physically and mentally; hence I went to my tent first among them. Just completed the account of our journey till now in the diary. I hope that tomorrow, we reach the house and fulfill our goal.

Ajay's Diary
November 20, 2010–11.30 pm

I am writing in this diary after a vacuity of two days, while sitting in my hospital's canteen. It is almost midnight and I am waiting for Professor Arya to call. The past two days have tremendously agitated me from inside out. There are no more words left to describe what has happened, but to plainly write the events down.

That night after I retired to my tent, I slept like a dead man having finished the diary. Again in my dream, the events of the past few days reiterated. My coming here in this town, amidst in this trouble was not worthless. Meeting Sawmya was a blissful event during the helpless and hopeless phase I was passing through.

Her executive talks, her ambrosial smile, her courtly appearance; all made me forget about the peril that was lurking. She never blanched to take any risk. I wonder where our new relation shall lead us to. Was it just the heat of the moment or something concrete to it?

I felt the warmth of her touch even in my dream. It made me feel serene in that forest. It provided an armor of insurance in the dark. *"Wake up, wake up"* I imagined her whispering in my ears. I was lost in her warmth. Suddenly, I realized the meaning of her words. I got up, opened the zip of my tent and looked all around. The lights of other tents were shut off. Everyone was calmly sleeping.

I reposed on the mattress again. Just as I did so, I wondered who was on the guard? After the event of last night, Rajesh Singh had appointed his constables to monitor the entire night, in shifts. While in bed, I looked outside again.

I saw Raghu sitting on one of the rocks.

He was moving to and fro, perhaps dozing due to sleep. I was about to close my eyes and fall back to sleep when I noticed something. *I saw the same shadow which I saw in my dream the earlier night.*

It was moving swiftly toward Raghu!

The apparition was getting clearer and clearer. It was the same female figure I saw hanging from the tree that night when my uncle was murdered. I was not dreaming this time. *It was real! It was the witch! The cold, dead witch!*

For a few seconds, I froze. I wanted to shout, but could not. It felt as if my throat was choked, my vocal cords were paralyzed. I tried to get up, but could not do that too, as if I had been nailed down by some external force. *Was I under her spell?*

May be I was! But, I just could not lie down there and watch the witch carry out her attack. I recapitulated the night of the uncle's murder when I saw her for the first time. I felt the same. In fact, I collapsed that night.

In my childhood, I felt the same whenever I encountered god-awful situations. Danger would make me freeze instantly. So, it was not something new or related to any kind of spell. It was my plain fear that was killing me, and I had to overcome it, overcome it faster! I rolled myself to one side and got, up and out. The witch was now very close to Raghu. Somehow, I could not amass the courage to shout or do something.

The witch was now just behind him who was completely unaware of his *kaal* a few inches behind.

Finally, I mustered all the adrenaline I had and was just about to shriek, when a loud sound shuddered me. It was that of a bullet fired in air by Rajesh Singh.

The witch was startled by that.

"Surrender yourself! Any move shall be your last one," Rajesh Singh roared.

Raghu had woken up from his trance. He culled his rifle. The other two constables also quickly targeted her with their respective guns. *But, the witch did not move an inch.*

It was still very dark in the forest to make out any distinct details of her. All that I could comprehend was that she had long black hairs that obscured her face absolutely except her left exophthalmic eye, which alone was enough to affright the soul out of any mortal body, like it did to me that night.

She was wearing the same black-bridal dress that everyone in each era had dramatically cited.

I looked at her feet to confirm if they were turned backward, as Manohar had described. But, the thick grass obscured them beneath it.

'*What would happen next?*' was the only thought in my blocked mind that moment. Was it somebody human in the disguise of a witch who had been trapped dearly and would now be revealed? If not, then why did it stop in front of the gun? Was it the end to the drama that was happening here in this town? Was our assumption of the witch, *false*?

She still did not move. Rajesh Singh announced again, "Put your hands above the shoulders and kneel down to the ground."

She waited for a few seconds and then followed the officer's command. The other two constables moved ahead with their guns aimed at her. Raghu was already standing very near to her.

My heart was beating very fast. My sixth sense was telling me that there was still more to it! Something terrible was going to happen. And it did!

When all the constables came close to her, the cries began again. But, it did not come outside of any window, somewhere distant in the temple or from the trees this time. It was indeed produced by her. As she neither moved nor did anything else, the gunned men did not get panic. But suddenly her mewls became very loud and *still louder*. Within a few seconds, it became so loud that we all had to steadfastly shut our ears. It felt so helpless that it was lofty to even stand erect on the ground. The policemen, including Rajesh Singh, had to drop their weapons. The situation had now anti-poled. *Everyone except her was kneeled down on the ground with their hands above the shoulders, on the ears.*

She corralled Raghu's neck, who was kneeling helpless near her. She twisted it and in one stroke, *it was over!*

Raghu's corpse fell down in front of us. On seeing this, his two counterparts, Mohan and Ramlal rushed toward her to avenge the cold-blooded murder. They made the most terrible and *the last mistake* of their lives. The witch in a similar manner grasped both of them.

"Spare them, you bloody demon!" screamed Rajesh Singh and picked up his pistol, despite the extreme acoustic trauma he was facing.

However, it was too late. The witch slashed their throats with her hands, or what was apparent now, *her claws*. She was indeed a witch, *a real witch*! There was no further mystery prevailing over her identity. *Three reckless murders just in a matter of thirty seconds, removed any bit of suspicion, if any, whether she was a witch or not.*

Rajesh Singh fired at her, but the bullet hit Mohan's body instead.

Her cries had stopped by then. Rajesh Singh leaped toward her in a rage, but the witch did not move. She waited in her place quietly for him to arrive.

We were at a considerable distance from them. Suddenly, fog covered us and we could not see what happened next. Rajesh Singh and the witch disappeared in a thick cloud of fog.

"What should we do sir? She will kill him too," I was anxious for Rajesh Singh.

"Don't go there. Just wait till the fog clears off. It is too risky to fight her, especially now, when you don't have any visibility," replied Professor Arya.

"But we cannot let him die like this, sir. He is such a brave and honest police officer. We must do something!" I replied and began to run towards them, but Professor grabbed me.

"Wait! If someone has to go in there, it shall be me," he said and in a moment, disappeared in that cloud.

Once in there, he lit up his torch and searched for him. The fog was dense enough to perceive anything. All he could have appreciated was the flicker of his torch shifting here and forth. *There was no word from him.*

"Sir! Are you alright? What's happening?"

There was no response from him for a few minutes. I decided not to waste any second and went ahead. Just then, I saw him emerging, alone.

"What happened sir? Where is Rajesh Singh, and the witch?" I asked.

"I could not find him. The witch seems to have dragged him away so that she could kill him with pleasure."

We searched for him for nearly an hour in every direction, but there was no sign of him or the witch.

Now I, Professor, and Ram veer were left alone in the dark. There was no one to back up for us.

The *Battlers* on whom we relied thus far, were gone. After several minutes, Ram veer stood up "Dawn is near sir, so is the house too. We must resume our journey. By the time we shall reach there, it will be full daylight. And the witch shall be not that sturdy in the day," he said and picked up one of the guns. "Sahib, shall I give both of you the other ones?"

He asked us simultaneously.

Professor said, "The guns couldn't save these men. What better purpose shall they serve in our hands? I am more comfortable without a weapon in my hand." I too agreed with him and chose not to acquire it.

We recommenced our journey with a great discontentment in our hearts. The witch had acquired an imperishable slot in my cognizance that was now impervious to relegate.

After another hour of walking, sight of the house appeared. It was as old creaky house. It looked as if it stood there at the mercy of nature for eternity. It's walls were black on the outside as if an attempt was made sometime to burn it down. But, the monstrous house resisted it by virtue of its evil powers.

If there was one place in the world that could house the witch, it indeed was a perfect one.

No living entity on this earth could inhabit it, but the dead!

I looked at a window on the first floor. It appeared to me as if some mystic eyes were watching us, though I could not be sure of anything comprehensive.

I looked at the entrance of the house. The front entrance door did not have any lock on it. It was open for anyone who could dare to walk inside.

While I was wondering, Professor almost reached there.

He turned toward us and asked, "So you guys want to come inside or stay out there?" The appearance of the house was too forbidden to enter. But, we came this far and lost our valuable men in the mission. Though it repulsed me to the core, I had to go inside. There was no turning back now.

I just wished that Ram veer's postulate that *'the witch is not so sturdy during the day,'* proves true.

Once we entered the house, we found ourselves in the middle of a large hall. It indeed was a house that was burnt in the past. It once housed exquisite interior that was now trying hard to express itself from among the soot that covered it.

From one end of the hall, stairs went up to the first floor. Professor said in a low note, "Be aware. The witch might be anywhere in this house. Though frivolous in daytime, she still might be strong enough for three of us. In any case, we have to stick together. That is our only chance if she attacks. Ram veer, can you handover to me my bag pack you have been carrying for so long?"

"Sure sir, it's all yours." He laid it down.

Professor opened it and took out a small instrument. It looked like an old radio that recently had been repaired. He switched on a button on it and placed it in one of the corners of the hall.

"If you are wondering what this is, then let me tell you. It is a machine that masks loud sounds. The sound made by the witch back there was much above the loudness discomfort level for any human being.

In my research on the myths about witches, I found it to be a quite common phenomenon among them. They produce sounds such a high intensity that our auditory nerve is not able to adapt quickly, and hence causes the *Brodman's* area; the sound perception center in our brain to be shocked.

That is why a person loses his composure for the time exposed. By switching on this device, a constant set of white noise is delivered within a perimeter of a twenty meters that will mask the loud sound, if produced again by the witch. Had I anticipated it earlier, those lives could have been saved."

He took out another instrument from the bag. It appeared like the device that diabetics use to monitor their blood sugar. He clicked it on. "It is an infrared thermometer. It will tell us about the presence of anything supernatural nearby. It can detect change in the environment produced by one."

"So what does it say about this hall?" I asked more with a tint of anxiety than that of curiosity.

"Not so significant here but," he moved it up over his shoulder "it points to some activity over there." He pointed toward the corner where the stairs were located. "Come with me."

We both walked behind him to the stairs. At the lower end of the stairs, he rose the device up again. There was definitely some fluctuation in the reading when he held it up.

He began to move up on the stairs and we followed him.

The stairs ended up in a hall, which too was deserted. There was a door on one of the walls that led to another passage. There was no lock on it. It was plainly latched. There was no streak of dust over it. It appeared as if it was open and welcomed us inside with a grin.

Professor signaled us to follow him to the room. He twisted the latch gently. It opened without a hitch as if it was used customarily. We entered the room behind him.

The room we entered was consummately dark. There was no hint of light in it. It was filled with a strange kind of aroma that I had never experienced earlier.

Ram veer lit up a torch. Professor also lit up his lighter. We were standing in another hall, much larger than the one on the ground floor.

There were strange kinds of symbols everywhere in the hall. Walls were smeared with the marks of nails all over. The marks extended way up on the roof. *On looking down, I realized that we ourselves were standing on another large and strange kind of symbol.* It appeared like a pentagon, but of a different kind. *It was inverted with a circle around it!*

There were different kind of articles placed in the center of the pentagon. There were few bones that appeared as of human origin, a small sword, a metal plate, a cup, and a stick.

Professor said, "*Inverted Pentacle, a traditional symbol of Witchcraft.*" He continued pointing to the articles,

"Typical tools used in witchcraft, *a paten, athame, wand, and a chalice*; each of which represents one of the four elements; *earth, air, fire, and water.*"

"What does it mean, sir?" I asked.

"*It means that we are standing right in front of the altar where witchcraft is done.*"

Suddenly, we heard the sound of a door creaking. However, it was not exactly the hall's door. It came from some distance.

"What is that sound?" I asked in a low note.

"I think it is the sound of the front entrance door. *Someone is here.*"

We were alerted by his words. We knew who that 'someone' could be. *It was the witch.* We had trapped ourselves imprudently in her house and that too in her ceremonial hall. It seemed as if there was no place to escape since the hall had only one exit.

We heard the sounds of footsteps, which were becoming more and more obvious. They were coming from the stairs to the first floor.

"What shall we do, sir? It appears that we cannot escape her."

He was calm enough to be terrified like me.

He signaled toward the large black curtains covering one of the windows. "We must immediately get behind the curtains. And Ram veer, keep your gun ready. We just might need it, if it all proves to be any competent."

"But she will find us there too, Professor," I said.

"I know, but there is nowhere else to go!"

We hid ourselves behind the black curtains.

The footsteps were moving closer to the door. She would definitely apprehend from the white noise and the unlatched door that all of us were inside, ready to be preyed upon!

What possible could we do in front of her? *Behind the black curtains, we were waiting for our black dressed death* in that black forest. My promise to Sawmya of returning back safely was just a curtain call apart to be crumbled.

CHAPTER 14

KALKIYANS

Ajay's Diary (Continued)

The unlatched door opened governably. The footsteps were now inside the hall. I wondered why Ram veer hadn't fired his gun. Was he waiting for a signal from Professor? If yes, what was Professor waiting for?

I tried to look at their faces. But behind the black curtains, in the closed space, I could not discern them.

The footsteps came to the center of the hall and paused. There was no sound for the next one minute.

She might be looking straight toward us! She might attack us anytime now!

The scene of *'in-a-flash murders'* of the three policemen hours earlier was looping repeatedly in front of me.

A thick layer of sweat camouflaged my entire body just in a few seconds.

Anytime her claws would cinch our collars. We were waiting just as guinea pigs in front of her.

Unless it was not her!

Unless it was someone else!

I peeped out of the curtain. I could not see anything, as it was very dark. The only streak of light was that coming from the open door. Suddenly, something lit up in the room. Was it the witch's furious eyes? But I did not see her. Instead,

I saw the silhouette of a man in the now perfectly lit room. The light came from a large candle that he placed in one of the points of the pentacle. He lit up another one and placed it in another point. And then another, till all five points were occupied. His figurine was now very apparent, as the room was luminous by now. I looked at Professor who was stupefied. It was as if he had seen a ghost!

He spoke softly, *'the librarian.'* I understood whom he was referring to. It was the same librarian whom both Professor and Sawmya met earlier. But, what the hell was he doing here?

Professor signaled both of us not to advance. Maybe, he wanted to observe his intent of coming here. Akbar, his name as told by Professor, sat down on the floor near the pentacle and took out a small book from the bag, he carried with him. He extracted several photographs and placed them in the center of the pentacle. Then, he opened the book and began to recite some kind of mantras written in it.

It was then that Professor beckoned to act. As we suddenly emerged from the curtains, Akbar was startled. Ram veer grabbed him from behind and pinned him down on the floor. He was ruffled to see us, but did not speak a word. Professor took the photos in his hand and showed them to me. It was of none other than us; I, Professor, Ram veer, Sawmya, and Kabir.

"What the damn are you up to Akbar?" I asked him.

"It is overt Ajay; he was going to perform a *witchcraft ritual* to cast a spell on us. Spell in the form of *the witch*. Like he has done previously in all of the murders."

Akbar, still pinned down, recovered from the shock and now had a stern expression on his face.

"Witchcraft ritual! I do not understand Professor, how is the ritual related to the killings? We just witnessed the witch herself murdering those men today," I was puzzled.

"'Yes, it was she who did it, but she was directed by this gentleman to do so. Don't you wonder why did the witch spare us after assassinating the policemen?

Or that night, when your uncle was murdered, why did she spare you? I will tell you why; she was ordained to do so. You can see these symbols and articles; as I said, these are the typical tools used in witchcraft. The evil force that is awakened by means of such craft shall follow the behest of the awakener and kill the victims targeted specifically. Now, you can see our photographs that he is possessing; *we were his next targets*. For such rituals, the presence of anything belonging to the target is a pre-requisite. Photograph, though do not fall under that category, still contain an impression of the person and can be apt for such ritual. Am I correct, Akbar?"

Akbar burst into laughter.

"Professor, you seem to be quite a reasonable man, reasonable enough to decipher things quickly and arrive at resolutions pre-nurturing in your mind. Now, if you allow me, shall I sit freely and talk? It is you three against one old frail man, who is like a sitting duck right now. I shall not be able to speak while your man is constraining my right shoulder. That is the weakest aspect of my body; *Frozen shoulder*, if you have heard."

Professor Arya decreed Ram veer to let him loose.

He sat catching his breath. Ram veer also sat near with his gun aimed at him.

"So shall we begin Akbar? Or you need some more air?"

He smiled at us and spoke, "I will not waste my time, Professor, as I don't have much. This forest was once inhabited by a tribe known as the *'Kalkiyans.'* Members of the tribe worshipped the yet to appear, tenth and the final incarnation of Vishnu; *Kalki.*"

They abjured the worship of all other incarnations of Vishnu, like Rama, Krishna, and other demigods. The Kalkiyans were also very well known for their practice of witchcraft. For them, it was a way of their life. Among them, there were few learned ones of the art who could perform the highest degree of witchcraft. They were known as *'Sarp Kalkis.'*

The Sarp Kalkis were also adroit in the art of *voodoo*, a dangerous ancient practice that stemmed somewhere in West Africa and subsequently spread all around the world. The practice is commonly referred in our country as *Jadoo-Tona*. The amalgam of voodoo and witchcraft made them one of the most fierce and feared tribes of their times. The neighboring tribes would not venture into their territory. Nobody would dare to take trouble with them, as they knew that one deadly spell cast by them would be enough to settle the score.

It is said that long ago, one of the neighboring tribes called 'Parvas' killed few of the Kalkiyans, due to land dispute. The family members of the deceased ones approached the Sarp Kalkis to seek revenge for them. The head of Sarp Kalkis cast a spell on the Parvas. The entire Parva tribe was affected by plague just in a week and in the subsequent week was wiped due to the rapid aggressiveness of the *Black Death*. Since then, the Kalkiyans lived boldly in their territory and no other would even dare to step on their land.

There was one more secret about the Sarp Kalkis.

They believed in the concept of an eternal spirit. According to them, after death, a spirit always hovers in the material world around the place of its death. It never leaves the mortal world. It was possible to ensnare it and make it reel back into the body. But that was not possible in case of any spirit. The spirit had to be specially blessed and pure enough to do so. In their entire history, the Sarp Kalkis had whacked it several times, but availed only in a few of them.

Once, the three-year-old son of the chief of Kalkiyans was playing in the jungle along with other children. Suddenly, a large snake appeared from the bushes. All the other children ran away immediately. But the chief's son fell down while escaping and hurt his leg. As he became an easy prey, the snake attacked him. At the same time, a young teenage village girl was passing through the jungle. She had lost her way through the jungle and had mistakenly entered the Kalikiyan's zone.

She saw the child being attacked by the snake and fluxed to save him. She intervened and blocked its path. The snake was enraged, and instead attacked her. It bit her multiple times, but she did not budge from her stand. Till then, the other adult members of the tribe had arrived. They asundered the snake away from her and lambasted it to death.

By then, the girl had lost her senses. They took her to their tribal doctor. By the time she was brought there, her heartbeat and breathing had paused . The doctor declared that she was no more. The news reached the chief of Kalkiyans; Saunikeya. He rushed to the doctor's house, eager to meet his son's savior. But on coming to know that the girl who saved his son's life was dead, he was struck with grief.

He immediately went to the head of the Sarp Kalkis; Vishvembar. He asked him to revive the girl by any means possible. Vishvembar told him that he would attempt it, but could not guarantee, as it was viable only in rare cases.

He, along with other Sarp Kalkis, performed an intense ceremonial to make the spirit retreat to her body. This time they were successful. *Her spirit was the purest of the pure*, *Vishvembar told.* He said that a spirit like hers would appear only once in a hundred years. He said that she was born with Lord Kalki's blessing and the Lord Himself macadamized the way for the ritual to be a victory!

Her fingers started to flicker and later, her entire hand. The warmth of her breath returned. Her heart began to pump blood to her great vessels again. *She was alive again!*

Her soul returned from the gallows to reinvigorate her body with a new vitality. *But, that blessing was not without a curse.*

It is said that once a spirit homecame in that manner, it was not possible to make it abdicate the body again. The body even if hurt to an extreme extent would not perish. There was only one way to destroy it; to burn it down, which Anand Swami and Uddhav Singh failed to accomplish.

Name of that girl was Maya! Maya, whom your town fears now as *The Witch.*

After being born again from her death, she led her life like a holy person, to prove her worth. She would always help the destitute. She was a faith healer. Mothers whose children were sick used to come to her to take her benediction, and it is said that the child would convalesce immediately once Maya prayed for him or her.

When she grew up, she started teaching poor children for free. It was due to her efforts that the underprivileged and downtrodden people of society could dare to send their children to school to get educated.

She would even pay money from her father's and later her husband's accounts to help a poor child sustain his education. *And look, what this land has given her back in return.* When Uddhav Singh and the goons were lacerating Maya in front of the entire village, not even one parent of those children stood up for her. She went through a gruesome and fake witch trial and the same parents watched it like a puppet show. They all believed in Uddhav Singh's words, when he declared that she was a witch and forgot all the congenial the same witch had done to their children. Some of them even screamed along with others, *'Kill the witch! Kill the witch!.'* Ungrateful bastards!

While she was being ached during the trials, the news reached Saunikeya. He, along with his men rushed to the village to rescue her.

They were too late. By the time they arrived, Maya had been buried in the grave behind the temple. But Saunikeya knew that she was not dead. Her spirit would not desert the body so easily. The same day, another woman had died in their tribe. In the late night, when all the priests retired to bed, they dug the grave and evacuated Maya.

She was alive, but in a horrifying state. Her body was almost burned completely except for her face, which was now not divine anymore. They put the other dead woman's body in the grave and took Maya along with them to their forest. Maya was in a half-conscious state.

Luckily, the Kalkiyans also found Maya's daughter in the jungle earlier that day! Thakur had sent his men to carry her to the jungle where they could kill her and dispose off her body by feeding it to the wild. However, few Kalkiyans saw her running away from the goons. They rescued her and killed the scoundrels.

Maya, though alive was as good as dead. Her physical condition was so heart trending that she was able to gain consciousness only for a couple of hours in a day. Her mental state was so obnoxious that she would not even recognize her own daughter.

During the time she was conscious, she would be in a rage. She just wanted to kill anybody that came in front of her, though she was very anemic to do so. To keep her restrained, she was kept in a separate room with strict supervision. This continued for several days. Unable to see any improvement, Saunikeya went to her room to ask her what was the reason behind her exasperation.

She told him that she wanted revenge on the rascals who brought her to this state. Saunikeya proposed that he and his men were efficient enough to kill all her evildoers.

But, she was adamant on killing them herself. In the frail state of hers, it was far from possible. "You once saved my life and blessed me with ascetism and purity. But as you have come to know, there was no use of the sanctity that you bestowed upon me.

Those bastards were elated to see an innocent woman being tried and murdered, her family being shamelessly executed. They should get what they want. This village should understand what a real witch means. *Please convert me into one.*" She begged to him with tears in her eyes.

Initially, Saunikeya was resentful to do so. He had seen the benevolence of her soul, the immaculacy of her heart.

Now, to turn her into an evil was something he was not amenable for.

But, it was the same benevolent soul on whom those demons performed their misdeed. It was the same immaculate heart they wrecked to such an extent that she became a walking dead. He could not sleep composedly in the nights to come, reminiscing of the gravest act of bestiality he had ever heard or seen.

And then, finally, one night the Sarp Kalkis on his request performed a ritual. The entire ritual lasted the whole night. To make her sturdy enough to annul her enemies, they had to infest her spirit with the spirits of ferocious demons. They summoned the demonic spirits and did the necessary.

The ritual took up a heavy toll on her body, and she went unconscious for two days. When she woke up, she was rapacious. She was now not herself, she was not Maya. *She had become what the people had accused her of. A blood-thirsty witch.*

The Sarp Kalkis announced that she was too dangerous even for them and could randomly kill any of them. Therefore, they kept her in heavy chains. To make her revenge a success, they would cast a spell on the offenders. In order to achieve it, they just needed a personal belonging of the target. They performed the art of voodoo on that belonging by casting the *witch's spell.*

Once the spell was cast, she would be liberated of the chains. She will kill her criminals, and then return back to the room.

All this continued till almost all the offenders, including Baldev Singh, Anand Swami, Uddhav Singh, and Tara were killed. Then, one day, when she did not have to hunt down anymore, she broke the chains and murdered one of the tribal men who came to provide food to her. The Kalkiyans was taken aback by shock. *The monster they created was now hunting them down.* Maya had gone *berserk.* The evil powers of the demons had overtaken the spirit of Maya. She no longer was any possessed woman who was taking revenge on her criminals. Now, she was a demon whose thirst would be quenched by killing anyone who came in her way.

Saunikeya believed that it was his misdemeanor that he saved Maya and transformed her into a witch. He was fervid to stop her by any means. There was only one way to do that since it was impossible to kill her directly. That was to expel the spirit out of Maya's body and make it enter into another human being. Once inside another body, the spirit takes time to overcome the native spirit.

During this time, the evil spirit is prostrate enough to be dominated. And destroying the body which it has just colonized, would inevitably expel the spirit out of it too, unless summoned back by another ritual.

He himself performed an intense ritual in which he forced the spirit of Maya to enter his own body because he considered it as his error. And while he still had some sense while her spirit was overtaking his body, *he slit his own throat.*

He forfeited his life and saved the tribe. As for Maya's body, it was burned immediately, so that her spirit could not return back to its native body by any means."

"But she did return, didn't she?" Professor asked.

"She did, Professor, she did! But before that you must know what happened to the Kalkiyans. In the years to come, there emerged another group, skimming from the scum of the Sarp Kalkis. They would never use their skill of witchcraft for their selfish benefits, but only for the good. They called themselves *Ashva Kalkis*.

Their occurred a series of dispute among the two groups, which now were clearly divided. The other neighboring tribes, which initially kept themselves aloof from their conflicts, now saw the opportunity to uproot the Kalkiyans once for all.

One night, one of the neighboring tribes, *Magara Daityas*, attacked and killed a large number of Kalkiyans, including Vishvembar. *It was the night of a massive bloodshed.* Only a few were fortunate to escape. Among them were the family of Saunikeya; his wife, his son, and daughter of Maya; Sharanya, who had been now adopted by Saunikeya'a wife. Also, a few members of the Sarp Kalkis and the Ashva Kalkis managed to evade.

They migrated to neighboring villages. Some of them settled in Jaisinghpur. Because they were now a sect reduced merely to a few numbers and were on hunt by the *Magara Daityas*, they disguised themselves among the villagers. They merged themselves with them as farmers. The Ashva Kalkis considered it as their fate and lived in accordance with it without any titillation of revenge. They focused on earning their living and raising their children well. They believed that it was not witchcraft, but education that they needed to foster them with.

However, the Sarp Kalkis would not sit dummied up. *They lived each day insatiated with revenge.* But without Vishvembar, they were anemic. There were no others left within them who were facile enough in witchcraft rituals to uproot the enemy. Their only hope was the son of Vishvembar; Vaaman, who was ten years old at that time. At a very young age, he started learning the art of witchcraft from his father. And later after Vishvembar's murder, Vaaman's conviction of perfecting it grew stronger. His mind was being regularly pumped with words of vengeance by the senior members of Sarp Kalkis. When he attained the age of thirty-six, he was capable enough to perform an extreme level of witchcraft, black magic, and voodoo. He was again admonished of his father's murder by the elders.

However, by that time, the *Magara Daityas* had grown into a large population. To destroy them, he would need a strong evil force, a savage monster, against which Magaras could not stand any match. *And there could not have been a more barbarous monster than Maya.*

But to make her operative again, he had to make her soul enter into a body that she would be familiar with. It was most condign for it to enter into the body of her bloodline. It was not hard for Vaaman to know the whereabouts of Maya's daughter, Sharanya. Sharanya too lived in Jaisinghpur with her two daughters. Vaaman performed a ritual and summoned Maya's soul like his father did once.

And it happened so. Maya returned back, all evil, all infurious after many years in her daughter's frame.

Maya, under the spell of Vaaman began to annihilate the Magaras. That was the second witch attack that nearly vanished the Magaras from the face of the earth. If they wanted, Vaaman and other Sarp Kalkis could have stopped Maya from further killings, as their revenge was now fulfilled. But they realized that Maya was a great potential they could use to expand their domain over entire Jaisinghpur and neighboring villages.

Maya began to hunt down the innocent villagers as well. On hearing the account of similar witch attacks, the Ashva Kalkis who had not indulged in witchcraft since long were now alerted. If they would not intervene, Maya would exterminate the virtuous citizens.

And then entered the scene, the son of Saunikeya; Pallav.

As Sharanya was the adopted daughter of Saunikeya, she and Pallav were brother and sister by relation. So in order to save the villagers and rescue Sharanya from the clutches of Maya, he attempted to decast the spell. But it was not successful. Now, the only way left was to kill Sharanya. With her death, Maya's soul would leave forever until summoned again.

But as she was his sister, and it was his conscience to protect and not kill her; he did otherwise.

First, he along with other Ashva Kalkis managed to murder Vaaman, so that he could not recall Maya again. Then, he did what his father did once to save others. *He infested Maya's spirit into himself and committed suicide.*

Maya was gone again. But till then, damage to Sharanya and family was done. The villagers had known that she was the witch who was out to kill them. So one night they gathered and surrounded her house. They burned it down. However, she managed to escape along with her daughters.

But that was not the end. Years later Vaaman's son repeated the history again. This time again, he was settled by Pallav's nephew.

Since then, the forthcoming bloodline of Maya undergrounded.

That was again futile. History has imitated itself several times since then and is imitating yet again.

In my humble opinion, Professor, I believe it should. For reasons, I told you that day.

And again, in my humble opinion, Professor, I believe that you should let me complete this ritual."

While listening to Akbar, we didn't realize that inch by inch he had come very close to Ram veer. He snatched the gun from his hand and pointed at us.

"On your knees! Everyone!"

We all were taken aback by surprise, but did not have any other option except to obey his command.

"So Akbar, you a Sarp Kalki, Vishvembar's bloodline! You are the one who has invoked the spirit of Maya and has got the people murdered by your evil ritual!"

Akbar laughed and said, "I thought you were a more reasonable man, Professor. Now, you all can leave the hall quietly and let me finish my job."

We got up and moved toward the door to exit the hall. While we were flaking off, Ram veer sprang back on him. "You bastard, I will not let you get us fed by the witch!" He grabbed Akbar's arm and tried to snatch the gun. But Akbar kicked him in his abdomen. Ram veer fell on the ground. Akbar pointed the gun to his head. "This is the last warning! Out you fool! Quickly!"

Ram veer was about to move when we heard a gunshot. We thought that it was all over. He had been shot and would die soon. *But it was Akbar, who fell down.* I turned around to see who had fired. It was more elated than surprised to find the answer. *Rajesh Singh! His bull's eye shot to Akbar's head through the half-open door pinned him down forever.*

CHAPTER 15

THE SARP KALKI

✱ *A* *lthough I had my diary notes to supplement the following account, I found ProfessorArya's tapes more befitting than mine.**

Professor Arya's Audio Tapes
November 19, 2010

I could not believe my eyes when I saw him.

Ajay too was ecstatic to see him alive. "We thought that you were dead, officer. Hence, we moved ahead. How did you escape?"

"Even I surmised that I was dead for a while. The witch did attack me, but I freed myself from her grasp and fled away. In the fog, I could not make out where I was heading. While running, I turned around to see her when I stuck a large rock and fell down. After that, I cannot conjure up much. When I recovered my sagacity, I returned back to the place where it all happened. But you guys had left by then. Thanks to the marks left by Ram veer, I reached here. In time, I guess?"

"Well, in time officer," said I. "If you had delayed a little bit, this crazy lunatic would have been successful in his ghastly intentions."

Rajesh Singh exclaimed, "Did the crazy lunatic tell you anything?"

"He did provide quite a treasured dossier but it is a long story. I will narrate it to you on the way back. We have to reach the town soon. Other people's lives are in danger, including Sawmya and Kabir. We must return as soon as possible. I think we have a lead that can help us."

I stooped down to take the gun from Akbar's hand. It was tightly clenched in his dead hand.

While abstracting it, I noticed that his right forearm bore a tattoo. It depicted a king cum warrior seated on a horse with a sword in his hand. Both the horse and the warrior were facing backward.

I instantly recognized it. It was the image of the prophesied avatar of Vishnu, Kalki. It confirmed that Akbar was indeed a member of the Kalki tribe.

"Professor, do you need a hand?" asked Rajesh Singh.

"No officer, it is done."

I handed it over to Ram veer, as Rajesh Singh already had one.

I also took the book Akbar was reciting from and secured it in my bag. There was no time to open it.

We were on our path again, walking hastily following the trail. The good thing was that we had marked the route and unclogged the bushes; hence it was taking less time on the way back. But even if we could go faster, still we could not escape the *one night* that was lingering around.

After walking for about two hours, it was dark again! From the incidents that occurred on the nights earlier, I had developed nyctophobia. But we didn't have time to set up our tents and sleep this time. Luckily, it was an unclouded night, so our path was well discernible. After another hour of walk, we were damn exhausted and paused for a few minutes.

We sat down on the ground. We took out some food and devoured it. I later realized that we had not eaten anything, the entire day. After finishing, we decided to relax for a while. Rajesh Singh got up and said, "I shall just have a round of nearby to see if there is any danger around," and left. Ajay kept trying his cell phone again though in vain. I took out the book, which I had gathered from Akbar's hands.

I opened it. It was a very old book, as if it belonged to the ancient times, written in pure Sanskrit. I warned myself not to recite it, which was my witless propensity while going through a book; as it might serve to arouse the witch.

But on turning few pages, I realized that it was contrastive to what I had contemplated. The mantras written in it did not mean to invoke any spirit or cast a spell. *Instead, it meant for protection from evil spirits!* It was meant for a kind of ritual that would negate a previously cast spell.

'I thought you were a more reasonable man, Professor' Akbar's words kept coruscating my now bankrupt brain, again and again.

Did he mean that my reason of assuming him to be a Sarp Kalki was wrong? He had the gun in his hand. If he wished he could have killed us all in an instant. *But he didn't.* Even when Ram veer attacked him; he still did not kill him.

The Inverted Pentacle! The traditional symbol of Witchcraft!

But Wicca or Witchcraft traditionally was never meant to harm people.

Instead, the witchcraft in earlier times was aimed to protect people!

'I thought you were a more reasonable man, Professor.'

He might have been a Kalkiyan but not a Sarp Kalki.

Instead, he was an Ashva Kalki! He was performing a ritual to negate the spell that had already been put up against us!

But if he was trying to salvage us, who was the *spell caster*? Who was the Sarp Kalki?

"What happened Professor, you seem to be lost? What is that book?" Rajesh Singh was standing in front of me. He was staring at the book with ambiguous eyes. "Is this the same book that lunatic was using to drive the witch upon us?" He took the book from my hand. When he did so, sleeve on his right forearm retracted upward, revealing the Kalki tattoo on it.

Rajesh Singh was a Kalkiyan!

But why didn't he apprised us of his 'Kalkiyan' identity earlier?

There could be only one reason.

He was the spell caster!

He was the Sarp Kalki!

He was going through the pages of the book pretending to be a layman.

"What's this book, Professor? Looks like in Sanskrit. Is it Bhagavad Gita or Mahabharata?"

"None of it officer, it is a witchcraft manual. But it is meant to protect from evil spells and not cast them. Sorry to disappoint you, but it does not fit in the hands of a Sarp Kalki!"

I made it apparent in one sentence. There was no point in playing the 'cat and mouse game' anymore.

Ram veer who was sitting beside me looked at both of us. He was smart enough to catch and arrest the situation. He pointed the gun in his hand at Rajesh Singh straightaway.

"Take out your revolver and put it down, Inspector Sahib."

"You fool! I'm sure you don't want to shoot a police inspector," he said with a grin. "Even if you escape the witch here tonight, you will still spend the remainder of your life behind the bars for murder of a police officer."

I grappled the gun from Ram veer and aimed at him.

"That we shall see officer in due course of time. Right now, you have a lot to confess," I said while firming my grip on the metal.

Ajay who was silent till now spoke, "I am stunned, officer! I regarded you as an honest and a brave policeman. Instead, all you have done is plot the cold-blooded murder of innocent people."

"You idiot, you point this gun at me! Instead, you should be thankful to me. You are alive today because of me. It was me who had restrained her till now from killing you otherwise you would have been dead the day you entered this town. And you others, don't you think that you too owe me. I could have easily shot you too much earlier on the way."

"Then why officer? Why did you come here with us when you already knew the secret of the witch? In fact, you yourself are that secret," I asked him.

"As soon as I came to know that you guys were planning to visit the forest, I knew that you would have outlined for the house. It was once the habitat of Sarp Kalkis that had been burned out by the motherfucking Ashva pigs. To perform the enduring witchcraft rituals, I needed a silent and secret place. That was not possible back there in the town. Hence, I resurrected it recently, single-handedly. This is where I would cast spell on the mules I intended to get rid off, using their personal belongings or photographs.

In the house, you could have ciphered my secret. Hence, I joined you, so that I can dupe you. But that sucker Ashva Kalki, Akbar, reached the house before me. He was going to use his wit to put an end to the spells all for once but glad! You guys bought me some time. Surprisingly, he did not brief to you about me! May be you would not have believed him either.

Yes, I am a Sarp Kalki! I am the direct descendant of Vishvembar, and hence, belong to the bloodline that performs extreme levels of black magic and witchcraft.

When I grew up, I realized what a prodigious society I belong to and what ominous potential I possessed! Having realized it, I felt moronic to live such a life; full of junk, like the others. I wanted to be ruler of the public, not a public servant. For years, I mastered the art that was the trademark of my ancestors, *witchcraft.*

I invoked the spirit of Maya, as it had become my family tradition. With the launch of the steel company of Jatin Shah, the future of this town seemed bright enough. With more employment, sooner, there would be more augmentation.

More schools, colleges, then universities. Eventually, one day, it would turn out to be a modern urban town, like others, and beyond my containment. *I had to strike at the right moment.*

I began with the murders of the three laborers whom everybody believed were taken away by some beast. I knew from the start that the Ashva Kalkis will suspect it to be *witch-killings.*

They will soon discover me and try to kill me, like they did to my forefathers. Hence, I let the witch first hunt them. Few of the farmers who were killed belonged to the forgotten Kalki tribe. However, the main obstacle was to get rid of their chief, the grandson of Saunikeya. I tried to erase him from the face of earth but he escaped the first time. The second time he could not. I think Ajay more than me, you are familiar with him."

"Whom are you talking about? I never knew any Ashva Kalki chief or member!"

"Ahh!! He would be heartbroken to know that his dear nephew has forgotten him so soon. *His name was Raj Singh Thakur!"*

"*What!*" Exclaimed all of us almost together. It was the biggest shock that Ajay received till now.

"What the hell are you saying officer! Raj Singh Thakur, my uncle belonged to the blood line of the Thakur family. He never mentioned about the Kalki tribe to me or even my mother. Was my mother too?"

"No! you and your mother are indeed the part of the Thakur family. Your grandfather Naresh Singh had only one child, your mother. He knew about the family history and the deeds of his father Baldev Singh. He knew that one day Maya would haunt him and maybe your mother too. That may ascertain the loss of any inheritant of the Thakur family.

Hence, he approached Saunikeya's wife, Kunti.

He appealed to her to bestow him with one of her grandchildren. That was the time when Pallav had sacrificed himself during the ritual to liberate Sharanya from Maya's spirit. His son was then three years old. Kunti handed him over to Naresh Singh Thakur who adopted and raised him as his own son. *Rudra was his birth name, renamed later as Raj Singh.*

While Raj Singh was in tenth grade, Naresh Singh was attacked and killed by the witch. It was invoked by my grandfather. He too wanted to rule Jaisinghpur. Till then, no member of the Ashva Kalkis, even his mother had ever contacted Raj Singh. But, Naresh Singh's death alarmed them. The witch was on a hunt! They had to do something briskly. When Kunti told him about the truth, he joined hands with the tribe and helped them to kill the witch.

My father, on account of his forefather's death, never dared to evoke her in his lifetime. But I was not a shirk like him. I wanted to be the mogul of this place, not a scum. Hence, I did not hesitate to summon Maya.

Once she came back, she did what she knew best, *hunting!*

As for you Ajay, I liked you. I knew that after Raj Singh is gone, you shall become the inheritor of his estate. And you and I could have together dictated this place.

My powers and your gleaming vision could revive this ghost town from the dungeons back to a perfect state. But you brought Professor Arya in the scene and spoiled my game. I immediately sensed danger, when he assigned you to dig up the grave. I anticipated that sooner or later, you and Professor shall come to know that the body lying in the grave for a century was not that of Maya, and subsequently other facts as well. Hence I had to cast spell on you. But there was another impediment in my path. Akbar, another member of the Ashva Kalkis, was using his damn gifts to protect you and your friends. Before his death, Raj Singh had taken promise from Akbar that he would armor Ajay and his close ones.

And he fulfilled it to his last breath. You fools did not realize it. He was going to perform a ritual in the house that could revert back the witch forever. But you made my life easier by foiling his divine intentions.

Now, since he is dead, there is no legitimate Ashva Kalki left who can perform such a ritual again. There is no other option left for you, but to wait as her target."

I spoke after listening to him for long, "I think you are forgetting officer, who is the target at the moment. If you do not stop the dire straits, you have created right now, I shall not hesitate to pull the trigger. People whose own life in the town is in a peril would not assay, how a policeman was killed in the jungle."

"You threaten me while standing on the verge of your death, Professor! Just to add to your wisdom, while I was away a few minutes ago, I auspiciously did cast a spell on you three fools!"

By the time he finished his words, Ram veer screamed.

The witch had grasped his neck!

He was trying his best to push her apart, but her clutch was strong enough. I tried to aim at her, but as Ram veer was obscuring her, I could not dare to shoot. While I was guesstimating of what to do, Ajay ran toward her. He idiotically tried to attack her. But with her other hand, she gave a harsh blow to him and he fell several feet apart.

The witch twisted Ram veer's neck and in a flash it was over for him!

I fired at her, but the bullet missed. Rajesh Singh laughed, "It is of no use, Professor. Bullets would not do any harm to her. She is Satan himself, standing in front of you. Be a sapient that you always try to pretend. Shoot yourself and die at your own hands."

I checked the cartridge, there was only one bullet left. Rajesh Singh was correct, I might ravage that bullet too. I had to take the chance of what was blazing in my mind. The witch was coming toward us. She was furious, breathing heavily, ready to taste some more blood. Ajay was still on his knees, half disoriented from the blow. I had to make a choice. I turned the gun away from her and shot, but not myself.

I missed this time too. I aimed at his head, but it hit his neck. The severe gush of blood indicated that it had hit dead at the carotids and that *Rajesh Singh would die in a few minutes from hemorrhagic shock.*

The witch staggered. She stopped in her place for a while, as if she did not know what was to be done next. My guess was correct. As Rajesh Singh told that after the death of Akbar, his buffer against the *'witch spell'* upon us terminated; there was also plausibility that after Rajesh Singh's death, his spell on us would adjourn too. The guess of my *sapient* mind proved to be true.

The witch howled for a few seconds and then, *she ran away from us.*

Soon she disappeared deep into the darkness. Rajesh Singh who was counting his last breaths, murmured, "You bastards... you bastards have saved yourselves as of now... but... but... you don't know what have you done... till now she was under my control... but now she is an unleashed demon!... there will be no longer any revenge... it will be pure terror your town shall witness! With my death, my dream of becoming a mogul is over... now there will be only one mogul... *The Witch...*"

I went ahead to abut his failing body. I raised his head up and said, "Officer, though you have committed ghastly sins, but I will still remember you as an honest and idol policeman. If you go in front of your Lord Kalki like this, he shall not forgive you. Tell me officer, tell me... *who is she?* Whose body Maya has possessed? She must be Maya's descendant. Where to find her? And how to stop her? You may be redeemed of your sins to some extent."

On hearing me his drooping eyelids got filled with tears. He perhaps realized in his last moments that he had committed the highest degree of malfeasance in invoking Maya and using her to kill innocent people.

Yes, he was once an honest and idol policeman!

Parents narrated his exemplar to their children. They would tell them that Rajesh Singh is a great man, and one day they should become like him.

He never kyphosed in front of the local goons or politicians. He always maintained law above all. To discharge his service without fear, he did not even marry, so that nobody could ever break him in the excuse of family.

All was fine before he realized the evil inside him; the evil that corrupted him, made him dream of becoming a mogul, made him kill the innocent.

And now, he would be remembered as a devil!

Now parents will tell their children that he was a bad man and they should not become like him. *What blunder had he committed!* Now, there was no time to correct it. His wet eyelids were sealing fast. He had time for just a few words.

"I am sorry... Ajay, my brother... our father... he will guide you," he said and closed his eyes, forever.

Rajesh Singh passed away, and left Ajay and us in yet another shocking revelation by his foudroyant words.

CHAPTER 16

MY FATHER

Ajay's Diary (Continued)

*M*y father! I had not even heard his mention in years together and now Rajesh Singh revealed about him. And he was not just my father, *he was our father! Rajesh Singh was my brother!*

I just had a faint glimpse of my father. He left us when I was just five years old. All that remained as a proof of his identity was an old photograph, which also I had not seen in ages.

Now I remember! I had seen him alive just a couple of days ago in Jaisinghpur. Those eyes! Yes, it was him! He saw me too! *That paralyzed patient in uncle's hospital whose private room I visited on my first day to the hospital. He was Rajesh Singh's father! He was my father!!*

Did I have a brother? I was too young at that time to remember anything.

All I had been told throughout my life was that my father left us alone for another woman. My mother went into severe depression due to that and later died.

I was raised up since then by uncle. He also never recited anything about my father. During the earlier years, I lived in Jaisinghpur with him. Later, I was sent to Mumbai along with Rahim.

Till now, I did not even care to find out whether my father was alive or dead.

And today, Rajesh Singh's last confession shook the ground I stood upon. *Whatever was the truth, I had to uncover it soon.*

Professor Arya tapped my shoulder.

"Ajay, I know that your mind is getting clobbered by so many questions. Only way to calm it is to find answers to them. And to do it, we have to reach the town soon. Now, it is only two of us left. If what Rajesh Singh vaticinated proves true, then Jaisinghpur is in immense danger at the hands of the witch, who now is malignant than ever before.

We must haste, as we have got no time to lose."

I almost did not listen to him. I just knew that I had to search my father and ask him why he pulled out of our lives.

We moved steadily in silence. The way was now clearer and our minds more determined to cross the jungle. We marched non-stop for the next six hours. When we stopped, we could see the dawn, the highway and our van.

I drove the van straight to the hospital. There was no thought coming to my mind other than to see him. We reached the hospital in another twenty minutes.

I got out and rushed to the first floor. Professor was behind me too. He was trying hard to catch up to me. On reaching the private ward, where I had seen him last, I saw that the ward boy was shifting a body out of it. Its face was uncovered.

It was him! My father! He was dead! His head was turned around!

The ward boy paused and wished us.

Professor asked him, "How did this happen?"

He answered, "Sir, around an hour ago we heard his screams. When we reached the room, I saw the witch. She killed SP Sahib's father. She jumped out of the window and disappeared. We were too scared. We thought she might return. Dr. Nirmal has checked and confirmed his death. He also told me that if *Ajay sir comes to the hospital, inform him immediately to meet me.*"

I had no feeling of remorse, but despair that I could not ask him now why he did so.

Professor held my hand and took me to Dr. Nirmal's chamber.

He got up immediately on seeing us.

"Welcome sir, please be seated. I hope you been informed about the latest incident at our hospital. Now even it is not safe from the hands of the witch. It is unfortunate that it was SP Sahib's father this time. I think he would arrive soon, as we had informed the police station an hour earlier.

However, there is something I have to give you. Around midnight, SP Sahib's father called me in his ward and told me to give this letter to you. He told me that you would be coming to look for him. Oddly, he said that he was not sure of being alive till you arrive. So, I needed to hand it over to you myself."

I was stupefied. *How did he anticipate that the witch would attack him? And how that I would come to search for him?*

I had no answers for that, but may be the letter did.

Dr. Nirmal rose and walked out of the chamber. I read the letter.

Ajay's Father's Letter

Dear son,

If you are reading this letter then you are well aware of several facts by now. Also, I am no longer in this stone-hearted world while you are holding this piece of paper.

Due to the instinctive gift that I have received from my ancestors, I have perceived that Rajesh is no more. His lust of power has finally crucified him. I knew it was bound to happen one day.

I also know that after his death, Maya has now become an unrestrained devil. And the first logical victim of her's would be none other than me. After all, I belong to the clan that has kept her in chains since a century and used her for their egoistic purposes.

Since I am paralyzed and weak now, it is the perfect time to kill me, and she knows it very well.

To be honest, I am not afraid of death. Instead, I wish today that she kills me soon because I do not have the courage to face you.

I know that I do not have any right to call you 'son,' especially after what I have done to you and your mother. I know that you have hated me on even the mention of my existence throughout your entire life.

I rightfully deserve your acrimony, but please allow me to address you 'son'; 'my son' for once, as I coveted for it throughout my life, whether you believe me or not.

If you still care to read further, please allow me to give my unworthy justification for everything I did, though you have the right not to acquit me even after that.

My marriage with your mother was not my first one. My first wife had expired few years ago, and I was living along with my only son, Rajesh. Raj Singh Ji was well aware of that fact.

When he approached me with the proposal of his sister's marriage, I asked him why he intended to do so, as we both belonged to two opposite clans, the *Sarp Kalkis* and the *Ashva Kalkis*; both of which had a long history of bloodshed between them. He told me that exactly was the reason he wanted to do so. By getting his sister married to the Sarp Kalkis, he dreamed of the age old war coming to an end.

I was unlike my father and grandfather. I would never use my hidden powers to carry out evil purposes; he knew it very well. That's the reason he told of proffering me.

I and your mother were happily married. Though initially, I had doubts whether she would treat Rajesh as a stepmother; she proved it false.

She loved Rajesh as dearly as his real mother did while she was alive.

After few years, you were born and brought even more bliss to our family.

With your birth, our family was complete. I used to thank god every day for the ultimate joy of the family that he bestowed upon me.

I and your mother being your parents used to take utmost care of you, but Rajesh being your stepbrother proved to be more than a blood brother. He would hover around you all the time. With him being around, we never used to worry about you. You too would never leave him. Your two-stooges group was indispensable.

Everything was perfect. Everything was so good in life.

Until that day!

Rajesh was fifteen, then and you were five years old.

Your mother sent me a message at my work place that Rajesh had not returned till four pm, whereas his school would end by one in the afternoon.

I ran towards home, leaving all my work apart. After I could not locate his whereabouts for several hours, I went to the police and registered a missing complaint.

Till next morning, I sat at the door expecting that he would return. But he did not. Instead, I received a letter. When I opened it, my horror came true. *Rajesh had been kidnapped by my own clan people, the Sarp Kalkis.* I was approached several days ago by them, requesting me to use my skills to recall Maya for fulfilling their evil purpose.

I plainly denied them, and conveyed that I would never repeat the same solecism my forefathers had done.

And that was the result of my denial. *The life of Rajesh was on line.*

However, I had firm certitude in my mind that I would never walk on that path which led to nowhere, but ruins.

I went to the address they told me to come. But, I was not alone. There were still a few people from the clan who were steadfast to me.

I never wanted it that way, but it had to happen. *Perhaps, it was destined to.*

Bloodbath, for the first time among the Sarp Kalkis. We outnumbered them. I rescued Rajesh and took him back with me to home.

However, the ghost of the incident was not over. During his stay with the kidnappers, Rajesh had learned about his ancestral background and that he was a part of the *special ones* of the Sarp Kalkis.

He repeatedly asked me about how to perform black magic, witchcraft, about Maya and other such things.

I always scorned him and warned not to indulge in such activities. But, he was not a child anymore whom I could have restrained easily. He was a grownup, misled youth who would not stop exploring his new adventure. He accidently discovered few books of witchcraft lying hidden in my cupboard. Without my knowledge, he read them and opened the gateway of hell for him.

My fears became worse, when I saw you one day sitting with him in your room, *reciting evil mantras.*

I knew it very well that Rajesh was unstoppable. No matter how much I would try to retard him, the blood in his veins would always remind him of what he really was. That was his destiny. But you were impeccant. At an age, when a child learns to chant nursery rhymes, you were chanting evil mantras. Your association with Rajesh was compelled to lead to you to become one of them; cruel evil men. And, I could never let it happen. A father could never let his son walk on the path of doomsday. Hence, one day I packed my bags and left the house with Rajesh.

I know what I did was not justifiable, but I had no choice. I came back here in Jaisinghpur and started working as a school teacher.

I requested Raj Singh Ji never to let you know why I did so, as the answer could have let to your reunion with Rajesh and you could become another Sarp Kalki. Hence, he fabricated the story of my betrayal to your mother.

I did my best to try to keep Rajesh away from learning the evil art, but he was way out of my hands. He was a brilliant student though. Through his hard work, he became a police officer, but the dark side always lingered around him.

Soon, he perfected the art of black magic. He would repeatedly pry about Maya. He wanted to know about the whereabouts of Maya's kins, so that he could repeat the dark history of our ancestors. But honestly speaking, I did not have any clue about them.

Then one day, I read the newspaper about the missing of the laborers and the discovery of their dead bodies a few days later. I knew the apocalypse had started. I warned Rajesh to stop the deviltry, but he had gone too far to turn back. Instead to stop me for further interfering him, he did this to me. He cast a spell that paralyzed and weakened me so that I could not stand in his way.

That day, when you came to visit the hospital for the first time, I recognized you. Through all the years, I had been visiting Mumbai to have a glance of you.

I told Rajesh about you. There was still an element of brotherhood left inside him. He promised me not to direct Maya toward you as long as he is alive. After all, you were his kid brother.

With his death, son, that guarantee is over now.

And with my death, I would no longer be around to help you by any means.

You have to help yourself and rescue this town from devastation. But son, you must promise me this, in any event you shall not resort to the dark powers, which our family is unthankfully blessed with. You should not try to test the hidden powers that I believe you possess. If you do so, you shall too become a demon like Rajesh.

You must fight Maya without becoming a Sarp, but as Ajay, a noble man.

First, you must diagnose the witch; the kin whose body is infested with Maya's spirit.

During his visit to the hospital, Rajesh once mentioned about her, but I do not remember exactly.

He told me that he discovered about her from the school, I used to teach in.

May be she is related to the school, may be a school teacher or a staff, I cannot point for sure. I am helpless that I do not have any clue about her identity. But remember one thing, she will come in front of you in disguise. Then, she will follow you. And then, she will hunt you.

To end this letter, I would again apologize to you my son.

If you think what I did was right, please forgive my ignoble soul. If you think that it was not, continue to hate me but please, do not give up on my name.

I was and I will always remain,

Your unfortunate father,
Ashok

On finishing the letter, I just sat there with it in my hands for some time, I don't know for how long; few minutes, may be an hour or may be even more. Professor was kind enough for not letting me restrict my emotions that were flowing down my cheeks. *The last time I sobbed was when my mother passed away; today it was for my father.*

He was correct; I hated even the mention of his existence earlier in my life!

He was correct; I shall continue to do so even now, though for different reasons.

For him loving me more than my mother, for scourging her for my sake, for depriving me of the tangibility of a son.

His body was shifted to the mortuary. The past two days had taken a heavy toll both on my mind and the physique, I definitely was in need of rest or else I would have gone insane.

CHAPTER 17

THE WOMEN IN MY LIFE

Professor Arya's Audio Tapes
November 20, 2010

It was blithesome to meet Helena after a long time. Kabir had arranged for her stay in the mansion itself.

"Hi handsome! Or should I say, Hi Professor! If you are more accustomed to that nowadays?" Helena chuckled.

"*Cummon*' Helena, stop pulling my leg! Now we are grown up guys, not college buddies anymore."

"I know that Shashank, I know that we are grown up guys and now only professional buddies. Hence coming straight to the matter, the results of the body you assigned me to check have arrived at my lab. That corpse belongs to a woman who aged fifty-four years at the time of death. She died of stroke. *Neither of that fits into the description of Maya, whom you went to search in that black forest,*" she said with a grin.

"So you are aware what is going on and why I called you here? Please Helena, don't get annoyed."

"I am annoyed Shashank and I should be. You never apprise me whenever you land yourself right in the middle of life-threatening settings. I admit that our affair ended years ago, but that doesn't mean that you'll keep on averting me forever."

Though, I and Helena joined the medical college aspiring to 'heal the world' together thirty years ago, my stay over there did not last for more than a year; thanks to that incident in the medical hostel. I left the college and followed my path in search for the dark secrets that the world obscured underneath it; *the secrets of the occult, supernatural, paranormal.*

Helena and I fell in love during the first week of the college itself and were going out together quite well even after I quit the medical world. But, I *realized* later that the kind of life I was living as an '*occult hunter*' was surmounted with risks every day. And it was not fair for me to get married and put someone else's life in jeopardy too.

Though I broke up with her, I never revealed my real intent of doing so. She was very choleric with me and did not even contact me for five years, after which our relationship resumed, this time though of mere professional friendship. As she had completed her Master's degree in Forensic Medicine and then joined the Medical Forensic wing of an esteemed investigation bureau agency; I needed her now more than ever before, to solve the stuck ups I would often find during the cases I encountered. *And this time, it was one of them.*

Ajay's Diary (Continued)

By the time we reached the mansion, it was late afternoon. On the gate itself, I was abreast by one of the servants that a lady has been expecting me since early morning. I regretted for not contacting Sawmya earlier in the day. She might be immensely perturbed. As I entered the living hall, I saw her sitting on the sofa with her back toward me. She appeared from behind a bit different, yet familiar since I left for the forest.

Those two days in the forest appeared as if two years passed by.

For the first time in the day, I felt a facet of appeasement, like a homecoming from the battleground. As I came near her, she got up in advance, perhaps heeding my footsteps. She turned around. I was aching to see that smile, which had now become the only ray of sunshine in my dark world.

Instead, I was white knuckled yet one more time in the last forty-eight hours. *She was not Sawmya; she was Anjana!*

Anjana came forward, embraced me tightly, and started to sob. I stood there with her snuggled to me, trying hard to accept that it was not an incubus.

She continued to cry, but my arms did not ally in echo.

Appreciating my cold heartedness, she released me after a minute.

She gathered herself and spoke, "I know Ajay, you did not expect to see me. Right?"

"Right Anjana, shouldn't you be somewhere else with someone else right now? Or have you come to invite me personally for your marriage?"

"You have all the ground in the world Ajay to speak as you wish. I deserve to hear the most raucous of words from you. I know what I did to you is far from an action that qualifies to even beg mercy for itself. But, I had no other choice Ajay at that time. I could not have let my father die in front of me. Perhaps, no daughter in the world would. Even if it meant sacrificing my true love."

"Then, why have you come back Anjana? What disparate is the sphere now? Or has the heart of Major Khushwant Ranjan changed?"

"The sphere is definitely disparate now Ajay," she paused for a moment, then continued, "Major Khushwant Ranjan himself is no more." She was almost into another burst of tears, but somehow held herself back; perhaps she expected another insensitive counter from me.

"How? I mean......when did it happen?" I cursed myself for a while for being malicious to her.

"The day before my marriage was scheduled to take place, he was bouncing vivaciously in my *sangeet* when he collapsed. First, everyone thought that maybe it was because he was drunk. But when he did not respond at all, he was rushed to the hospital. *The doctors declared him dead immediately.* He had a cardiac arrest, they told me.

With his demise, the obligation on me to marry the one he had chosen for me also ended.

I discussed directly with him; Ranveer, about the matter. I told him everything about us. He is a decent human being. He accepted the fact that if I could not be happy with him, there was no point in the marriage.

I took the next flight after that and went to Mumbai. But, your flat was locked. I tried several times on your phone for two days but it was not reachable.

Then, I came here with hope to find you. I arrived here today morning, but your servants informed that you have gone on some expedition. They acquainted me with the current scenario of this place. That is so frightening what is going on here! They told me of your uncle. I am so sorry Ajay. I know he was to you, what my father was to me."

I was asterned. What her father did was not legitimate; but he fostered her and according to him, did what he thought was superlative for her.

"I am too sorry to know that Anjana. Although, I have abhorred him from the core of my heart for taking you away from me; I can fathom today very well what it feels to lose a father."

"Ajay, I know I cannot exonerate myself for what I did to you, but I know that I still love you. Please forgive your Anju. Let us erase those dark four weeks from our memory altogether. The years we lavished building our dreams together can outnumber those silly days."

She embraced me again. This time my arms could not resist. *Yes, the time spent with Anjana was the most glorious time of my life.* I realized the momentousness of it, after I lost her. Had it not been for that call by Kabir that night, I would have perhaps ended my fustian life soon, without her.

I was lost in her arms, as if nothing queasy happened earlier. We were deported back to the past nostalgic moments. With my closed eyes, I recapitulated the sweet memories that we cherished together. It was like it happened today. It was like we never separated. It was like I never went through that hellish phase. It was like I never got that call by Kabir and never sat out for this place. It was like I never took that flight and boarded that bus and never met... Sawmya!

But I did meet Sawmya, and I did fall in love once again! And I did love her even now! I opened my eyes to awaken myself from the nostalgia. *And I saw her! I saw Sawmya!* No, I was not daydreaming anymore! She was standing at the entrance of the living hall, perhaps since...I *cannot say when!*

I eased off my grip on Anjana. "Sawmya, when did you come?" Anjana too relaxed her shoulders and turned around with almost an equal dismay.

"I came a few minutes earlier, to learn if you are alright. It seems you are! Now, I should leave." She left instantly. I could hear the faint sobs that she was trying to hold back, but could not.

"Sawmya, wait! Just wait for a moment!" I almost shouted, but it was of no use, she was gone. I could hear the engine of her car setting into ignition.

I turned toward Anjana and said, "I acknowledge what you have done Anjana. But, you must understand that things are different now. I apologize to you, but you are too late in your redemption. I have to go now." I turned my back to her and walked out of the house. Whether I was doing the right thing or not, I did not know. I only knew that *Sawmya* did not deserve the antipathy in love that I tasted once at the hands of Anjana, a couple of weeks ago.

I took a car and left for Sawmya's house. She already had a lead over me and would reach her destination before me. While going to her home, I passed the spot on the highway, where we had entered the black forest. All the events related to that place clicked again in my mind. That was the same point, where my car got stuck that night while I was returning from Sawmya's home the first time; and the first time I saw the silhouette of the Witch on the road.

But where did she come from? Was she following me? If yes, from where? That night I returned from Sawmya's house. The words in my father's letter ran through my mind,

"She will come in front of you in disguise. Then, she will follow you. And then she will hunt you."

She did come in front of me that night! She was disguised! She opened the door for me! Then after I left from her house, she followed me on the highway. But she was unable to hunt me, due to Akbar's spell.

"May be she is related to the school, may be a school teacher or a staff, I cannot point for sure."

I knew who the witch was; who was the last descendant of Maya!

"... because I was worried about my aunt. She is a school teacher there in Jaisinghpur."

I called upon Sawmya's number, but she did not pick up. I tried again, but without response this time too. I left a voice message, "Sawmya, please do not go to your aunt's house. I think, *she is the Witch!* Maya has possessed her body. And she is more evil now. Please stay outside!"

'Will Sawmya listen to my message in time? Or has she already reached the house?' were the questions running in my mind at the speed of a bullet train in Tokyo.

I drove as fast as I could toward her house. While still at a distance from it, I could see Sawmya parking the car in front of her house. She walked toward the main door. I wished so hard that she pick up her phone and listen to my message before I could get to her. She looked at her phone and kept to her ears, but at the same time, the door opened.

I saw her aunt appear at the doorstep. Sawmya was jubilant to see her. But her aunt did not respond. She simply turned around and walked inside. Sawmya entered behind her and shut the door. In a matter of a few seconds, I too reached the house. I left my car and ran towards the main door.

I found that it was locked from inside. I wondered what might be happening inside. I did not want to alarm her aunt, so I gently pressed the bell and waited for a minute.

When nobody opened the door, my heart beat rose faster. I pressed it again, this time harder. It was the fifth time when I realized something was damn wrong. Then, I heard the screams of Sawmya. *"No aunt! Please leave me!"*

I ran to the other side of the house in the hope that I could enter from somewhere. Her screaming was getting louder. I shouted, *"You damn witch! Leave her; she is your niece! Have some mercy!"*

I ran to the backyard where I saw one of the windows of the kitchen open. I entered the kitchen and rushed to the direction where the screams were coming from. I searched the living hall and the bedroom, but could not find her. Moreover, her screams had ended. I rushed toward the first floor and stumbled upon something on the steps. *It was Sawmya!* She was lying still on the steps.

I held her in my arms. Her neck was not twisted like others, but she was not breathing either. I pressed my head to her chest. Her heart was still kicking. *She was still alive!*

I parted her lips and covered them with mine, giving mouth-to-mouth breathing. But there was no response. I could not feel the warmth of her breath that I encountered the night we made love. I began to pound her chest, and then again gave some breaths. After multiple attempts, she finally moved. She opened her eyes. *The warmth of her breath reverberated.*

"You came Ajay! I knew you would come!"

"I will always come for you Sawmya. I love you, and there is nobody else in my life, except you."

I tried to lift her up, but she moaned, "Aah! Be careful... my neck... it seems to be broken... what happened here?" She said after a pause, "Oh my god! My aunt! Ajay... my aunt... is the witch! It is aunt whom Maya has bedeviled! Aunt is the descendant of Maya!"

She opened her clenched fist. It had the mini bottle locket that I had given to her before leaving for the dark forest. Its cap was opened. The holy water that Rahim gave me once, proved its sanctity.

"This thing saved my life. I sprinkled it upon aunt while she was about to break my neck. Had not been for it, she would have taken my head off the body."

"I know that now. I know it is a big jolt for you as is for me too. But don't worry. We will take care of that. First, you need to be shifted to the hospital."

I dialed the emergency number of my hospital. The ambulance arrived soon. The paramedics lifted Sawmya gently and transferred her inside the ambulance. I accompanied her to the hospital.

She underwent an X-ray of the neck. Dr Nirmal placed the film on the X-ray board and said.

"She is blessed enough to survive paralysis or even death. The fracture is just limited to only half of the second cervical vertebra. Had it been a little more extensive, it would have damaged her spinal cord resulting in a grave injury. With this degree of injury, she should recover in another two months. Till then, she has to wear a neck collar."

I shifted Sawmya to a private ward. By then, Professor Arya and Anjana too arrived.

I told Professor about the incident. On hearing that Sawmya's aunt is the witch, he said, "Rajesh Singh was correct. After his death, the witch has become fractious. If she can attack her own niece, whom she had not even touched till now, we can just guess what she will do to the town people. Her identity is not a mystery anymore; hence she will no longer remain hidden. She may attack with all her pleasure now.

Ajay, can you come outside for a while? It is better that we let her rest."

I kissed Sawmya on her cheek and told her, "I will be back soon."

I turned toward Anjana and looked in her eyes—those same eyes that I used to get lost while looking at, once upon a time. But that did not happen now. "Please be with her for a while if you don't mind."

She smiled and said, "I will take care of her. You need not worry. What is dear to you, is dear to me too. Just be cautious."

I moved outside the ward with Professor and a heavy heart. *Was I doing any injustice to Anjana?* She had broken up her engagement and come here to be one with me. *She never ditched me!* She was simply trying to fulfill her role as a good daughter, like my father. He too did not desert me. He was just trying to fulfill his part as a good father, keeping me away from Rajesh Singh; keeping me away from becoming a Sarp Kalki.

"What are you thinking Ajay? You seem to be lost," Professor said.

"Nothing sir, nothing serious."

"Don't be reluctant to share with me what's going inside your head, Ajay. I know these are the most taxing times you are going through; all the strange revelations about your past, and now this new strife. I can see that you are standing at a junction and do not know which way to go. You probably have your doubts equally about both ways. But give time a chance. If time has driven you into this state, it will drive you out of this too soon. Nature always finds a way to the most apposite by itself.

You must let yourself move with your natural instincts without any remorse for anyone. Right now, you must focus on something that is more important. The lives of all your loved ones are at risk as long as they are in this town. I can sense that it is the silence before the storm we are in that moment. Be prepared for the worst to come as, *it will come!*"

"I agree with you, sir. I am not now longer perturbed with what I have been through, but what the people close to me are going through. I just want them to be safe and sound."

"If you bother so much about them, then they shall be alright. Now, let's get serious. It is already getting close to night. If the witch has to attack, she will do it tonight. We have to fasten our seatbelts for that. We know that there is no potential member of the Kalkiyans left who can stop the witch. As for you, your father and uncle did not want you to become a tantric for good reasons. However, there must be some other way to fight her. Do you remember your uncle giving you any clue to do that?"

"No sir, there was nothing of that sort foreshadowed in his letter.

Of all the last conversations I had with him, he instead negated the witch theory behind the murders. He acted as if he was never aware of the past and present happenings."

"Did he tell you something in the past? He might have broached you about these dark times, which were destined to come."

I stressed out my mind, but could not get anything remunerative out of it. I had few glimpses of the time spent with my mother, her death, then coming here to live with uncle. While I was a child, Rahim really took abundant care of me. When I grew older, I was sent to the city to pursue better education. Rahim had accompanied me since then till now. I had, in fact, spent more time with Rahim rather than anyone else. He played the role of my mother and father simultaneously.

I remember once when I felt very sick, after returning from a college trip. A few hours after arrival, at my apartment, I felt excruciatingly nauseating. I vomited blood minutes later. And that wasn't a single *episode. There* were several further ones of hematemesis in succession. I was admitted to one of the best hospitals in the city. But the doctors could not help much.

After a battery of tests they could not diagnose my ailment. I had lost so much blood that I was being transfused daily to stay alive. Raj uncle visited me at the hospital. He was gravely worried. I remember now the short conversation that took place between him and Rahim while I was half asleep in my private ward. Initially, due to the frailness of my mind during the sickness, I considered it to be extraneous, but now it seems very pertinent.

"I am sure it is *voodoo*. Those *Sarps* willed to take him away. They wanted him to blend into their demonic society. But I warned them from doing so. I threatened them that I would not spare anybody if they tried to do so. Now, since they cannot have him, they have cast *'Raktamrityu Mantra'* on him. He will soon die of blood loss if you don't act, Rahim. All these doctors, medicines and transfusions would not save him. Only you can do so. You must get it done tonight itself."

"Sahib, I swear I will not let those suckers take away Ajay baba from us, either in life or in death. Those Sarp Kalkis are truly like their name. Like a snake, they want to eat their own child.

Tonight, I will perform the craft I have feared all my life. I never wanted to kill anyone, but these fucking pigs do not leave me a choice, Sahib."

He said and then he left the room. Uncle came and sat close to me. He gently touched my head and whispered, "Don't worry dear. You will be soon alright."

And it proved to be true. The *'bloody episodes'* terminated the next day. With further transfusions, my hemoglobin improved rapidly. I recovered well within a few days. The doctors credited themselves at that time, but now I know who my healer was.

"It is Rahim," erupted from my subliminal mind.

"What?"

"Rahim; my guardian, my angel. He's been with me throughout my life. He is probably a very strong representative of the *Ashva* Kalkis. That is why uncle entrusted him to me. He has been my watch guardian and protector all throughout my life. It is so deplorable of me to have ignored him. The poor fellow had gone to visit his ill wife, and I did not even call him once. Had it not been for him, I would not have survived that witchcraft attack that I was subjected to. I am very concerned about his wife."

"She is alright baba." A voice came from behind.

I turned around.

Rahim was walking towards us!

CHAPTER 18

NIGHT OF THE WITCH

Ajay's Diary (Continued)

I jounced with joy, "*Rahim, you are back!* I am so glad to see you! I am apologetic that I never queried about your wife. How is she?"

"She is fine now. It was what I anticipated. Someone had cast a spell on her. In her dream, she saw a witch and got paralyzed due to shock. It was a plot to keep me away from here, so that I could not be around you. In due course of time, she recovered enough to speak, and the first words she spoke were, *go and protect Ajay baba.*

I am here, baba, and shall not leave you until death. Also, I need to tell something about your family history. Raj Singh Ji had steered me not to disclose it to you but..."

"I already know Rahim what you intend to tell me. That I am a *Sarp*, and you are an *Ashva Kalki*. I wonder what difference it would have made had I been apprised of the truth much earlier. At least, I would not have lived my entire life in the dark."

"It was your uncle's disposition. And I believe he was justified. He always wanted you to live in a lucid way. The knowledge of your true potential could have nuked you like it did to your brother."

"You knew that Rajesh Singh was my brother? And did uncle too?"

"Yes baba, we knew that Rajesh Singh was your brother. In fact, your father always admired your uncle and named *Rajesh* after your uncle's name, *Raj*."

"Rahim, please help us if you can. What can we do to barricade the witch? With Rajesh Singh's death, it seems that danger has aggrandized."

"Not just danger, baba, expect hell. Tonight is the 'New Moon' night or the *Amavasya*. It is the time when any evil power manifests itself in its unrestricted form. That is what the prophecy is in my village. But don't worry. I will not let the witch hurt you. She has to step over my dead body before she can even touch you."

"It is no longer about me Rahim; thousands of lives in this town hold more merit than mine alone."

"You speak like Raj Singh Ji, baba. He surely would have been boastful to see you; if alive today," Rahim sighed.

Professor interrupted us at the moment, "Rahim, you stay with Ajay tonight. He might not care for his own life, but it indeed is very important for every one of us. The town has already lost its leader, and there is no one to scout it. Once these tough times are over, it will need another *Raj Singh* to lead it to enrichment and prosperity. I am going to Sawmya's aunt's house to find any clue that might possibly help us against her. Till then, you all better wait here in the hospital. Have a watch on Sawmya too. The Witch might return to hurt her again."

"Are you sure sir, you need to do this? Going there alone can be suicidal. After all, it is where she lived all that time while simultaneously murdering people. You better take Kabir or someone else with you." I was floored at his decision of going alone in there.

"If at all I encounter her, it will be my fate. The presence of Kabir or anyone else would not make any difference in what is destined for me," he replied adamantly.

I knew there was no point in altercating with him. By now, I understood two facts very well about Professor Arya. First, he was a *self-assured man*; not afraid of taking risk. He perhaps had been through similar situations earlier too. Second, he was *a lone warrior*. He preferred tasks to be done alone. I knew that given a chance, he would have stoutly gone to the dark forest alone in search for the witch!

"That's alright sir, but please do take care. Right now, this town needs you more than me as its guardian."

"I will Ajay, I will," he replied and left the scene.

I was contended to have such a nervy man standing beside me in the frustrating times I was going through.

It was close to midnight. I and Anjana were sitting near Sawmya's bed. She was sleeping peacefully, thanks to the sedatives given by Dr. Nirmal. He deemed it necessary, as she had passed a hell lot of physical and mental stress that day. I was anxious about Professor Arya. He asseverated that he will return back to the hospital before the midnight hour. However, his absence till now spiked new fears in me. I tried several times on his phone, but every time the *'not reachable'* reply would deject my soul. I blamed myself for not coercing him to take someone along with him. Visiting the Witch's own house, that too during the midnight hour, was something nobody else could have dared.

I looked at Anjana. She seemed to be dozing. Then, I looked again at Sawmya. I cursed myself for parking the two women in such an awkward situation. I did not know what would happen in our matter, but it was sure that I would never forgive myself for breaking an innocent heart.

I left the room and came out in search of coffee. There was a small canteen in the hospital premise that was open twenty-four by seven. I sat there and continued with my notes in the diary, while waiting for Professor.

Ajay's Diary
November25, 2010–8pm

It has been five days since I wrote in my diary. I am exhausted of exclaiming my pathecities every time I begin with it. Hence, this time I shall write; just write *one last time.*

Back there in the hospital canteen, once I was finished with my previous diary notes, I ordered a cup of coffee. I bewailed for not having asked Anjana to accompany me. Maybe, I was trying to desist her. Just when I took the first sip of coffee, my phone rang. I prayed it be that of Professor. *It was!*

For the first time, his tone was very apprehensive.

"Where... where are you Ajay? Tell me quickly!"

"In the hospital canteen; what happened sir?"

"Where are the others?" He *shooted* before I finished my reply.

"Rahim is sleeping in the doctor's duty room, where I arranged for him; Kabir and Helena should be at the mansion and Anjana is in Sawmya's ward."

"Listen Ajay very carefully. Stand up and run towards the ward."

"But why? What happened?"

"Run with the phone on your ears. I will tell you on the way."

I was too confused by what he meant. But, since I trusted him blindly now, I did exactly the same.

He continued, "In that house I came across an album, which was the family album of Gayatri, Sawmya's aunt. According to that album, there is no evidence that Sawmya or her parents whose picture is hanging on her wall are related to her anyway. I also came across an official paper, which clearly states that Sawmya was adopted by Gayatri from somewhere else. The origin of her parents is unknown. Later, when I was surfing through Sawmya's stuff in her chest of drawers I saw a schmatte in it, that *black-bridal dress.*"

"What do you mean to say sir?" I arrived on the floor where her private ward was. I saw her room door from a distance. I raced toward it.

"On further search of the house I reached the basement, *where I found Gayatri's body.* Ajay, what I am going to say is formidable for you. But it is... the bitter truth that..."

By that time, I opened the door. Anjana rushed and embraced me. "...*Sawmya.....is the Witch!*" Professor completed his sentence.

I looked at the bed. Sawmya was sitting on it, but the way she sat made my heart jump into my mouth. *Her head was facing backward.* Her two feet were twisted like what I had heard since childhood, the typical description of a witch. Gradually, her head reverted to its anatomical position. Her hairs were scattered all over her face. Her eyes were furiously red. Her skin was no longer beautiful; it was charred, as if burned recently.

"Such a big cheater you are Ajay Singh Thakur! You left the girl you fucked for three straight years to die at the hands of a witch. Chhhhh... so bad!"

Her voice had completely altered. It appeared as if there was someone else speaking in her. Then, I realized. It was not Sawmya anymore. I was standing in front of *Maya*. The clock had struck twelve in the night! The prophecy in Rahim's village turned out to be true. Maya had now full possession over her host. *To my ill fate, the host was Sawmya.*

"And why are you crying, you whore?" she said, looking at Anjana, "Didn't he told you about the ecstasy that he derived in fucking me was much greater than he got from screwing you. Am I incorrect Ajay? That's what you told me that night before you left for the black forest!" She went into a burst of laughter with that.

"Sawmya, please wake up. I know that you can listen to me despite this demon inside you. Do not let her overpower you. You are a strong woman, you can do it."

"Ha! ha! It is too late for that Ajay. Your dear Sawmya is no longer in this world. Her body is now mine and mine only." She laughed again for a few seconds, and then suddenly started to cry. Her neck twisted again backward. Then, looking at the open window, she murmured, as if she was speaking to the entire town.

"You... you gang of scoundrels! You all were watching my death like a drama. All of you knew that it was a false plot to justify my rape and then murder. But... but none of you came forward. You all enjoy seeing a witch being tried for her crimes. You all love witch trials, don't you?

Well, tonight I will give to you, your favorite entertainment. You all shall see a witch trial, as you have never seen in your life before and shall never see after. Because, none of you shall remain alive to see another.

This shall be *the last witch trial.*"

Her head turned forward, and she vomited almost a gallon of blood.

Anjana fainted on this horrid scene. Rahim entered the room by this time. He screamed at Maya, "You bloody Witch! Don't you dare to touch Ajay Baba? I will tear you into pieces if you even think so."

He lunged toward her with a small trishul in his hands.

I grabbed him from behind.

"Stop Rahim, do not hurt her! If you kill her, Sawmya will die too!"

"Leave me baba, if I do not kill her right now, she will not leave anybody!"

On hearing us, Maya laughed again, "Oh you foolish Kalkiyans! I am so jaded of you. You insignificant motherfucking pigs think that you can kill me. Come, kill me! Kill me if you have the balls!"

This infuriated Rahim even more. He got out of my grasp and dashed toward Maya. Before he could reach Maya, she clutched his neck, and then gave a strong blow to his head. Rahim fell down on the floor. She cantered upon him and nabbed the trishul. Rahim was perplexed and did not know what to do. Then Maya did the horrible. *She inserted the trishul in his eye sockets and scooped his eye balls!*

While he was screaming in excruciating pain, she inserted the trishul in the left side of his chest and wrenched it several times.

In a matter of seconds Rahim's flickering body became still.

She got up and stood right in front of me. I looked in her eyes. Behind those red-threatening eyes was somewhere that girl whom I met that night and fell in love with. I had promised her that I shall return from the forest safe, so that our love could escalate further. *But I had returned to witness her in this state!* Now, there was nobody to stop the *Maya* in her from fulfilling her thirst of my blood, she awaited for so long.

She too stared straight in my eyes. *What was she waiting for? Why she was taking so long? Was Sawmya still alive in that corpse?*

She said sullenly, "Ajay Singh Thakur, the great-grandson of the His Highness; the ever motherfucking bastard Baldev Singh!

Baldev Singh—the man who arranged for my gang rape by those filthy men. The man who immodestly murdered my loved ones. The man who affirmed to the world that *I was a witch.*

Do you deserve such a clean death?

No!

I shall not kill you. Instead, I shall spare you with a regrettable life.

The people in this town, who will remain alive after tonight shall spit on your face and urinate in front of your mansion, when they will learn that you are responsible for what happened to their family members tonight. Tonight is the night I had been waiting since a century. There is no longer any motherfucking Kalkiyan to legislate me. Let me be the first to have the pleasure." She spat on my face and micturated on the floor.

Then, she turned around and jumped out of the window.

I stood there, as if struck by a thunderbolt for several minutes.

Soon, the hospital staff gathered outside.

Night of the witch had begun.

Anjana regained her consciousness an hour ago. She was too scared to come out of the room. I insisted her on leaving the town, but she firmly denied it. She said that she would not leave me now, no matter what happens. As she had committed that error earlier, she would not repeat the same. Rahim's body was shifted to mortuary. Professor Arya arrived fifteen minutes earlier.

As for me, I was still awestruck by the entire episode. *Why it had to be Sawmya? Why did every time life has to be impartial to me?* If I could have deciphered earlier that Maya had invaded Sawmya, maybe I could have saved her.

I still could not believe that it was Sawmya, who followed me that night on the highway while returning from her house; it was she, who I saw on the night of uncle's murder hanging from that tree; it was she, whom we encountered in the forest and who killed the policemen.

I could not even believe it was Sawmya, who's such a monstrous form I witnessed an hour ago and who killed Rahim in front of my eyes.

I was also feeling guilty that I saw all that happen to Rahim in front of me, and could not do anything. The man who raised me, the man who placed his life on the line to save me, the man who meant almost everything to me; died such a helpless death and I stood there, watching like a sheep.

Professor said, "Sawmya being the host of Maya's spirit is a shocker for me as well. I am very much disappointed that I could not discover it earlier. You called me here with a great expectation to solve the mystery, but the mystery has solved itself. And, it's too late now."

"It is none of your fault, sir. You have done your best till now. Only due to your endeavors, we could reach the crux of the truth. I do not know what is going to happen next, but whatever happens, I do not have the courage to continue without you."

Kabir entered the room, he was in clear panic, "There is bad news Professor, hell has broken loose! Hundreds of women, most of them adult, are behaving in a very eccentric manner. They appear to be in a state of frenzy. *They have declared themselves to be witches!* They are ambushing men in their family and are dragging them somewhere. They have suddenly become extremely vigorous and beyond anyone's control. They even killed several men trying to stop them. First, it began with a small group of women, belonging to a locality, but now this hysteria is spreading like a virus in the entire town. On the way, I' have seen several such women coming here. Very soon they will be inside the hospital."

I asked Professor, "What is happening sir? Is it Maya?"

"Yes it is. The women are under her spell. It is a lesson she wants to teach the people. When a century ago, she was subjected to the false witch trial, nobody came forward to save her. This town has seen innumerable fabricated witch trials in which hundreds of women have been killed based on false accusations. Maya's case was not the only one.

Those dead women cannot come back to demand justice, but Maya is different. She has been impregnated with many demonic souls. She was branded and killed as a witch. Now, she has the possession of not only Sawmya but also of all those women.

She identifies herself as a witch and by using them intends to kill the men, as in men she sees her butchers.

If it happens there will be no men left in the town. And once the women come out of their delusion, they will die out of regret for killing their husbands, brothers, fathers, and sons!"

"It will be apocalypse sir! It will become the land of the dead. We must do something immediately!"

"First, we must do something to save ourselves," he said looking out of the window.

I came closer to him and saw outside. *At a distance, I could see a group of around twenty women marching towards the hospital with axes, knives, and daggers in their hands.*

My heartbeat ran faster on seeing this, and perhaps everyone's too.

Dr. Nirmal was in the room with us.

"Sir, even we escape, we cannot leave the patients to die."

Professor asked him, "How many patients do we have in here, doctor?"

"Almost forty. Many of them can be shifted somewhere on trolleys, but twelve of them are in the ICU. They are on ventilators. If we detach the ventilator even for some time, their countdown to death might be a very short one," replied Dr. Nirmal.

The women were very close to the hospital. Soon, they were going to be inside if not interrupted.

"Gather your staff immediately doctor, we do not have much time," Professor said.

The main entrance to the hospital was locked with a heavy iron chain. The women started to beat it violently.

Though the chain was strong, the manner in which it was trembling with each hit; it would not take long to shatter down.

That was exactly the idea of Professor. He wanted to buy some time till the chain would break. *And within few minutes, it did.* The women slammed open the gate and rushed in. They first went to the general ward. To their dismay, it was empty. Looking puzzled at each other, they then rushed towards first floor where private wards were located.

They searched each ward, but left empty handed. This made them madder. We were watching all this in the security room from the CCTV footages. However, I was concerned what would happen if they moved to the ICU that was located just the floor above, where all patients were shifted?

It was Professor's gimmick. Since it was not possible to extricate out the patients who were on ventilators, the only logical step was to shift other patients inside the ICU that was spacious enough.

But, it could become a death trap soon, as the frenzy women started to move towards the upper level. Then, began the second and most important part of the strategy, this time executed by Ravinder; a ward staff who has been working in the hospital since its foundation.

He volunteered for it. Just when they were about to step on their way toward the ICU, Ravinder emerged in front of them. He shouted, "Come and catch me sisters if you can; I am not afraid of you," and instantly ran away from them. This infuriated them and they chased him like a fox.

The women had become so crazy that they would surely tear him into pieces.

However, Ravinder volunteered correctly. He ran swiftly and led them away from the second floor.

Soon, he landed up in front of the O.T. complex. He opened its gate and entered inside. Just on entering the O.T. complex, he put on an oxygen mask that was connected to a mini oxygen cylinder that he carried in his arms. He turned on the knob of the cylinder and entered into one of the theatre. The women too entered inside behind him. But they could not find him. It was very dark in the theatre, as the lights were already turned off.

Ravinder had already made his exit through a small window that was used for passing surgical instruments and gowns from the autoclave room directly into the theatre.

For the women, it was a strange feeling in the room. The air they breathed in was *different.* They suddenly felt a sense of extreme dizziness. Before they could apprehend, the nursing staff placed a large iron bar between the handles of the *theatre* door on the outside. There was no escape for them. They banged the door, but the iron bar was too staunch to give away.

"Are you sure this shall work Professor?" It was again his idea to somehow trap them inside the O.T.. One of the nurses had already turned on the knob of the anesthesia machine several minutes ago so by this time *Halothane*, a volatile anesthetic drug had concentrated in the theatre.

They started to fall one by one. Within seconds of entering the O.T., they were knocked out.

"*I bet it did Ajay,*" Professor replied with a devilish smile on his face.

He asked Dr. Nirmal, "How long shall they remain like that, doc?"

"Given the concentration of the drug they have been exposed to, perhaps the entire day."

"That would be good enough. Now, open the doors of the theatre. I don't want to put their lives at risk, as they all are virtuous."

"Sure sir, do not worry about that," Dr. Nirmal said.

Patients were shifted to their respective beds. The deluded women were shifted to one of the largest wards and its door was locked from outside.

CHAPTER 19

THE LAST WITCH TRIAL

Ajay's Diary (Concluded)

I hugged the Professor, "Well done sir! I could not have featured such an intelligible quick fix to such a mingled situation. Frankly speaking, I have given up everything on you. Now, I am undaunted that you will surely get us out of this horror."

"That time will tell, Ajay. Now, without lavishing any second we must move to save the others. I can guess where Maya has taken them; the *Kali temple*, where she was tried and murdered. Kabir, where is Helena?"

"I am sorry Professor, but... Helena too has confederated the crazy women. She even attempted to kill me, but I escaped somehow," Kabir said.

I could remark cold sweat on Professor's face on hearing this. There was more to their relationship than we all knew. But he hid his anxiety underneath, the next moment.

"She must have gone to the temple too. We all must haste Ajay, there is no time to waste."

When I, Professor and Kabir began to leave, Anjana intervened. Looking at me, she said, "Don't you understand when I tell you that I don't want to commit the same error again. How can you go without me?"

"Anjana, it is too dangerous to come with us. You have just witnessed for yourself those lunatics who are under Maya's spell. They are thirsty for blood. They were just twenty in here, out there they could be in hundreds or thousands."

"I don't care Ajay. I cannot hide here and let you go alone. Remember, we promised to each other once that only death could do us apart. If I have not been turned till now like them, probably I would stay the same later as well. By pretending as one of them and mixing in their group, I could be of some help." There was doggedness in her voice.

"May be she is right Ajay, we might need her help. I do not think she accompanying us shall be a great threat to her," Professor said.

Though I utterly disagreed with Professor, I didn't want to defy him either.

On our way to the Kali temple, there was complete chaos. It was as if women in entire town had turned into *self-frenzied witches*. Men were trying to escape but those 'witches ' were too durable to let them go. They were dragging them towards the temple. Those who repelled were slained on the way itself.

It was like the scene from a typical zombie movie where a virus affects the entire town and turns people into the living dead. The only difference was that here only women were the ones being turned and men were the prey.

Suddenly, a pack of women surfaced in front of our car. Kabir who was driving hurriedly applied the brakes. They slammed the front mirror repeatedly and it shattered into pieces. Before we could realize, one of them grabbed Kabir's collar.

She was Helena!

Professor yelled, "Stop Helena, please stop for god's sake! You don't know what you are doing!"

But, she was completely spell bound. She pulled Kabir out of the car. Professor quickly shifted to the driver's seat. He put the car in reverse gear and backed it for several feet to get it away from the mob. Kabir was being stamped up by Helena and other women.

"We must save him, sir, or else they will thrash him to death." I feared for Kabir's life.

"Don't worry, I will not let anything happen to him." He pushed the speed paddle into full throttle and then acquitted the brakes. The car leaped forward like a missile. It went ahead and hit the mob. I knew he did not want to hurt them but there was no other way left to save Kabir.

Helena was hurt too. She fell on the ground and became unconscious. Professor got out and pulled her up in his arms. "I am sorry Helena, if that hurt too badly," he murmured to himself.

He put her on the back seat next to Anjana. She was startled to see Helena next to her.

"Don't worry, when she wakes up, she will be out of trance," Professor said, *acumening* Anjana's fear.

I abetted Kabir to the car. The mob was gathering again. We screeched the car through them toward the temple.

"Are you alright Kabir?" I asked him.

"Yes sir, just never have been handled up by so many women in my life," he smiled despite being badly hurt.

"You are lucky to escape dear, I have been at the receiving end of Helena too around thirty years ago. I was knocked down by just one hit of her's. She is indeed a superwoman," said Professor.

Soon, we were close to the temple.

The scene outside was bloodcurdling.

There was a large gathering of women who were kicking and shoving men into the temple premise. We stopped our car at a good distance from the temple. "Well, it seems absurd to make a direct entry in there. The mob will tear us apart if we try so, maybe we have to search another way," Professor said.

I said, "I know of a way sir. I saw it on the day of exhumation of Maya's alleged grave. There is a creak in one of the walls in the backyard of the temple. We can manage to sneak in. It leads near the barn, where the grave was located."

We drove the car while keeping it at an appreciable distance from the *witches*, to the backside of the temple.

Professor told Kabir, "Kabir, I want you to stay in the car with Helena. Until she is out of her senses, she will not be able to defend herself and we cannot carry her with us too. Call up the police station and inform them about the Kali temple. If you see any danger approaching, just start the car and leave. I do not want Helena to be in any further trouble because of me."

"Ok sir," Kabir never questioned any body's decision. He always complied it.

I, Professor and Anjana entered the temple premise through the creak. Fortunately, there was no action in the backyard. From a considerable distance, we could see the scene inside the main temple premise. It was unlike anything I could have figured.

Men who had been captivated were bound by ropes to pillars in the temple.

There were hundreds of women inside who all were under some kind of hypnotism. They were gurgling , "*Burn them, kill them! Burn them, kill them!*" while swaying back and forth.

Several of the men captured were pleading to women who were supposedly their family members. One of them was pleading to his wife, "Laxmi, please free me from the ropes. If something happens to me, then what face will you show to our children?"

She replied, in her trance, "If I leave you, you dog; you will go around and rape some innocent girl. Then, you will emblem her a witch and kill her! Men like you do not deserve to live on this earth. *The only place that suits your filthy existence is hell!*"

It was as if Maya herself was speaking through her.

Then, she continued to murmur, "*Burn them, kill them*" swaying in her position.

Suddenly, they all became non-vocal. I looked around and understood the reason. Sawmya or should I say, Maya, entered the main premise. On seeing her, all women came down on their knees and bowed to her as if she was a goddess and they were her devotees.

Maya spoke, "The time has come; the time has come my sisters. For centuries, these dogs who call themselves as '*Men*' have been crucifying us in the name of 'witchcraft.' They raped us, killed us, and laughed, standing on our corpses. We did nothing apart from getting subjected to their animal instincts time and again.

But not anymore!

Tonight, we shall put all the shame we have been subjected to, to an end. These pigs have derived immense gratification in accusing us and piloting us to false trials; but tonight, it is they who shall be put to *the trials*."

All of them started to chant together, this time louder, "Burn them, kill them."

Maya continued, "Bring forth the scoundrels."

Several women appeared from inside dragging Swami Madhusudan and few of his disciples. They shoved the priests ahead and tied them too to the pillars.

Swami Madhusudan exclaimed, "'Leave us you witch, otherwise God will not spare you! You shall rot in hell if you try to kill his servant!"

"Hell! Hell is what I have brought for you in this temple of yours, Swami. You goons have cheated the entire society since the inception by posing as the tickets to heaven, as the sons and avatars of god. Now, it is time to prove it. Let me see, which god comes here to save your fucking souls tonight. You are nothing, but demons in the skin of priests, encumbrance to the society. But do not worry my dear Swami, I will not be unfair. I will let you undergo a fair trial, like the one you put to an innocent widow, a few days earlier."

From the mob emerged Savitri, Manohar's widow of whose trial I was a witness.

She came forward with a jug in her hands.

"You need not guess Swami, what's in it," said Maya.

Her voice suddenly changed into a coarse one. It was similar to the voice of Madhav Singh, the witch doctor who conducted Savitri's trial and was killed later by Maya. She repeated what he had spoken earlier with a twist,

'Cow's urine is considered to be holy water in our religion. It is even accepted by modern medical science to have tremendous healing properties. Crores of Hindus use it regularly all across the country and even abroad.

So for any pious Hindu it may not be great deal to consume it. But for a demon it is impossible to do so. If you are able to drink one liter of it without vomiting then you'll be released. If not, then it'll be proved that you are a demon and shall be punished for being one.'

Savitri marched toward Madhusudan. On seeing her come towards him, he screamed, "You bitch! Don't you dare come close to me. Don't let that shit come close to my mouth or else I will kill you!"

Savitri grabbed his jaw and forced the jug's content down his throat. Swami Madhusudan vomited the entire urine instantly. Then, she forced all disciples to drink the same. Everybody followed the footsteps of their reverent guru.

Madhav Singh's theory proved to be false.

"Demons! Demons! Demons!" shouted Maya and following her, all women gathered inside. "A demon you are Swami and so are your pets," pointing towards the disciples.

"And in this holy temple, a demon has no place. In fact, he does not have any place anywhere in this world. You nasty demons, you will be burned in hell right here, right now."

Swami had broken down by now. He and his men knew that there was no chance of escape. In a few minutes, Maya would do the same that years ago was done on her by his ancestral guru, Anand Swami.

He craved to her, "Please forgive me, please forgive me Maya. What happened with you was an absolute injustice. But you have already killed your criminals years back. I was not even born at that time! Please do not punish me for the sins I never did. As far as *Savitri* is concerned, I was misled by my disciples. They convinced me that they have strong evidence that she is the executioner of her husband. If someone deserves to be punished it is them, not me. Please let me go. "

"What the hell you are speaking Guruji," said one of the disciples, "when did we tell you so? It was your plan to brand Savitri a witch, punish her and gain everyone's adoration. We acted as mere puppets in your hands. It is you, who was the mastermind of Savitri's trial and several others before!"

"Shut up all of you!" Maya screamed at them petulantly.

"Priests like you are pests on the earth and need to be disposed. You can go and argue about each other's infringements while stinking in hell together. Right now, it's time to disinfect this temple off your black souls. Bring the holy water to clean the mastermind Swami and his loyal puppets."

The women brought several canisters and put each one in front of them. On unscrewing caps of the canisters, *the smell of kerosene filled the atmosphere.*

They emptied the canisters over them. Swami and the disciples were completely drenched in it.

"What should we do sir; she is going to kill them!" I asked.

"I guess there is hardly anything we can do Ajay, but to wait for the police to arrive. I hope Kabir has informed them by now."

Maya walked toward them with a firelight, on the sight of which, the pleads of the priests winged. They shuddered to the core, "Please leave us! Please leave us! Have mercy!"

She stood in front of Swami Madhusudan and set him on flames, *"Mercy is what I forgot the moment I was branded a witch, you sucker."*

His screams echoed loudly in the temple, where once his fake sacred chants used to.

Then, she moved to each pillar and lit up his disciples on fire.

"We cannot wait like this, sir; we must do something. Next, she will burn the others too. I shall go in front of her and get killed rather than hiding here like a chicken," I was getting feverish.

"If you do so, it will be of no use. You can instead effectively stop her," he replied. I did not understand what he meant by that.

"'But how, sir? Though I am a Kalkiyan by blood, I am not versed with the Kalkiyan skills. I regret today for having not known to what clan I belong to. May be like Rajesh Singh, I could have restrained Maya and sent her back."

"Then let Rajesh Singh himself do it!"

"What! But he is dead sir. We saw him dying in front of us. His body might still be decaying in the forest or banqueted by the wild animals."

"Right! But his spirit is not dead. It is still wayfaring, stung with guilt of invoking Maya who has resulted in destruction of this town."

"How do you know that?"

Professor said, "In my years of encounter with the occult, I have come to learn few hidden arts. One of them is *planchette*, the art to recall a wandering spirit and to infest oneself with it, momentarily. It is a universal practice that many people attempt, but only few are successful. In one of my rendezvous several years ago, I came across a group of people who were successfully using the *planchette* to recall spirits and forecast future. They taught me that. Unlike what one has heard or read in stories, it does not require any sort of table, candles or coins. It can be done with a secret mantra anywhere, anytime. I believe it is the right place and the right time."

"But, what happens if Rajesh Singh's spirit does not pull out of you," I was worried for him. He was risking his life for us.

"That is quite possible Ajay, but there is no other way," he said and walked away from us in a corner. He sat down and murmured a few words.

After the fire had calmed down, Maya announced, "My dear sisters, now it is turn to kill the other demons. The demons you have caught from your own house. The demons, who stay with you day and night; the demons, who torture you right from the birth; some even kill you before you are born. As long as these demons walk on this earth, there will be more of us being accused of witches. *Hence, we must burn them alive!*"

The women brought more canisters of kerosene and emptied them on hundreds of men trussed to the pillars. The men begged them not to do the horrible, but the women were spell bound enough to listen anything. They took firelights in their hands and walked toward their husbands, fathers, brothers, sons!

What mistake a few men had committed a hundred years ago, today entire 'Men-kind' was going to pay.

"Kill those men—the scoundrels, rapists, murderers. They do not deserve to live." Maya was swirling at her place and screaming in all her madness. Suddenly, someone grabbed her wrist and stopped her lunatic dance. She turned around to see who dared to do so. It was the Professor standing boldly in front of her.

"You bastard! You dare to come here and stop me! You think that you will breakout from here?" Maya charged toward him. Professor caught her other wrist too and twisted both of them. She screamed in agony.

"I left you lose for just a while and look what you have done, you nasty bitch!"

She realized that she was now standing not in front of Shashank Arya, but Rajesh Singh.

The *planchette* had been successful. *Rajesh Singh was back!*

"How can it happen? You were dead! This same Professor killed you in front of me in the jungle." Rajesh Singh slammed her down to the floor. "Well, he brought me back too. Isn't he generous my dear lady?"

She got up back on her feet and said, "You are too late, Kalkiyan, I am too stark now for you to handle. You have made a great solecism by coming back to this material world. I will put you and this fucking professor together to a death, you could not have ever imagined."

It appeared as if the hold of Maya on the women alleviated as they interimed for a while. They stood in their place with a vacant look. They stared at each other and at their men. It was as if they were in the midst of trance and verity, and could not decide what to do.

But they did not deposit the firelights down either, which connoted that they were not yet out of their hypnotism.

Meanwhile, Maya grabbed Rajesh Singh's neck but Rajesh Singh chanted few words that made her step backward.

"By the power of our Lord Kalki, I condemn you, you evil soul to leave this body, and go back where you came from! Leave this girl alone. She is your great-granddaughter. Get out of her body and exit this world forever. We, the Sarp Kalkis gave you life when once you were gnawed by that snake. It was our mistake; we should not have interfered with nature's law. And then, we made a much bigger mistake by exploiting you to spread terror. We were deluded with power and brought ignominy to humanity. But tonight, all shall end. There will be neither any evil Kalkiyan like me, nor any rancorous soul like you wander any longer in this world. I will take you along with me to hell where we truly deserve our places. I command you to come with me!" He chanted few mantras in an ancient language of which I had no clue.

That thorned Maya. "No stop! You cannot do this! You cannot do this!" Rajesh Singh continued his chanting and that put her in a debilitated state. She was down to her knees, squeezing herself as if she was feeling extreme pain. "Stop, stop, I am burning! I am burning!" she said and then collapsed down to the floor. And, so did Rajesh Singh.

I was worried whether the chants of Rajesh Singh had merely driven Maya out of the body or killed Sawmya too! Professor got up and angled toward us. He said, "It is done!

Rajesh Singh and Maya have gone. Now, there is no need to worry."

I and Anjana walked towards him. I was very glad that the apocalypse had been forestalled and the town was safe now. I was anxious to know what happened to Sawmya. As we moved toward them, I noticed something cynical. *The women still appeared to be in a state of delusion.* They should have dropped the firelights, but they did not. Instead, they were returning to the same hysterical state.

Behind Professor, Sawmya got up on her feet. This brought some relief to me, but it did not last long. She picked up a firelight and hit it hard on Professor's head. He fell down immediately.

He was bleeding from both of his ears. The blow had perhaps ruptured the vessels of his brain. Sawmya, or to say *Maya* was laughing loudly. Maya had rooked Rajesh Singh of exiting Sawmya's body. She was still present inside her! The hard blow had probably killed Professor, so there was no chance of Rajesh Singh coming back.

"Poor Kalkiyan! He left alone. *May his soul rest in hell.* Now, it's time for you, great-grandson of Baldev Singh to join your idiot friend." Maya snatched a knife from one of the women and rushed towards me. I froze at the moment and could not move. The death of Professor had slivered me absolutely. I was not aware when Maya came near me, swung the knife and struck me. I just fastened my eyelids. *I didn't feel any pain, maybe I was dead with that blow.*

I opened my eyes. I could see her and the surroundings as well, and I was not dead for sure. I was not even contused. Then, I felt someone sinking at my feet.

It was Anjana! She, as my cover had got herself stabbed by Maya. She was bleeding copiously from her chest. I bent down and took her in my arms. I kept both my hands on her chest to stop the blood from gushing out.

"What have you done? What was her fault?" With Anjana racing to death too, my world had ended.

Maya hitched for a while.

"What was the vice of all the people you killed? Nothing!! Absolutely nothing!! You hypnotize these women, make them kill the men in their family.

Why? Because a few men raped you, stigmatized you as a witch, and killed your father and husband? Are you not imitating the same? You also have successfully stamped women in the town as witches. These men whom you are plotting to get killed, are they not somebody's father and husband?

Do you realize what will happen when these women will come back to their senses? When they will come to know what they have done, there will be no other option left other than to jump in the well and die. There will be no other choice left for them, but to kill their children rather them letting them grow up realizing that their mothers had killed their fathers. *What kind of retaliation is that?*

If what my great-grandfather did to you was a horrible sin, let me tell you it is no match for what you are going to do. Lord Kalki saved your life when you were bitten by that snake, but you have abashed him too. You have demeaned his name even before he has materialized in this world.

You want to take revenge? Then come and kill me! You have already killed Baldev Singh and all his descendants, then why leave me? Kill me, but leave these crimeless men. Accusing and torturing a woman as a witch is a social evil and should be condemned. However, with this act of yours, people's benignancy toward such a woman shall end forever. They will either fear or kill her, but none shall assume it to be a false allegation."

"*Enough!!*" Maya screamed. It was so loud that it literally shook the temple ground for a while.

It was as if a hundred people howled together. I replayed what Akbar told a day earlier. It was not just Maya, it were the hundreds of demons her soul was infested with. Maya was as innocent as Sawmya who herself was possessed. Now, the demons inside her began to reveal themselves, "You have spoken enough and we have heard a lot. Now, it is time for you to die." She raised her hand once again in the air that grasped the knife.

"*No, don't kill him. He is inculpable.*" I heard that voice for the first time from those lips. It was unlike anything I had heard before. It was a nectarous, genial and comfy female voice; but it did not belong to Sawmya either.

It was of Maya! Maya—the pure soul. Maya—the daughter, wife, and mother.

I glanced at her eyes. It was as if I was looking a hundred years back. She was a young, amorous, idolatrous woman. Then, why did it happen? Why it had to be her? She was robbed of all her immaculateness that day.

Yes, she wanted revenge! She wanted to kill all those who did this to her. Anybody would want that, no matter how pure. However, what she did later was not under her ascendancy. It were those demons who killed the others.

And now, they would not leave her. They committed murders of innocent people through the ages, not she.

She stood there with the knife in her hand, her hand raised up but still. I could not make out what was happening. Maya had locked herself inside Sawmya's body. Perhaps she was struggling with the demons, trying hard to convince them not to kill me. But why? I had no answer to that. She herself was completely still, but her eyes were not. They were trying to signal me something. They pointed to the knife in her hand. It was as if she was instructing me to take advantage of the break and do it!

But I could not do it, just could not! My hands became so numb, as if they were never there. And it wasn't any witch's spell; it was my worst fear standing in front of me. My one move though would have killed and got rid of Maya forever; it also would have killed Sawmya, the girl I loved. To save the town from the disaster, *I had to kill Sawmya with my own hands!!*

I just could not!

All the events that occurred since I met her, replayed live in front of me.

'Excuse me, is anybody coming here?'

'Hey! Are you lost? I'm so sorry to hear about your mother'

'And to call me you need to have my number.'

I just could not!

'Thanks for the flattering. So are you single or committed?'

'And yes, I do already have someone in my life.'

'He's there since I met him on that bus stand in Delhi.'

I just could not!

'I love you too my dear.'

'I wish I could join you. Now I shall wait for you here.'

I just could not!

I turned around and started to walk away from her. As I did so, my eyes went straight on all the men who were tied to the pillars, waiting for their death. Soon, this town would be filled with orphans who may not figure out what happened on this day.

Why did our mothers kill our fathers? Why did they later hang themselves out of guilt? All they would be left with shall be nothing, but a mocking future. They would lead the life of an orphan as I had, but may be worse as everyone did not have an angel as their guardian, as I had in the form of uncle. Everyone did not have a caretaker so loyal who would give his life to protect them, as I had in the avatar of Rahim.

'In all circumstances, Maya should be stopped! She must be'

'This is the reason I called you here Ajay. To save this town from burning in hell. That is my last wish. And I know you would fulfill it.'

Maya's hands began to flicker; her facial expressions were becoming stern again.

"Kill him! Kill him! He is the fucking great-grandson of the pig that raped you and murdered your family. Do not leave him alive!" The demons were overpowering her soul again. Soon, it would be too late to do anything.

I walked straight to her and snatched the knife from her hand. Just as I did so, her other hand grasped my neck. *The demons were back!*

The clamp of her hand was becoming firmer and firmer, I was already feeing anoxic.

"You son of a rapist and a murderer! I should have killed you long ago!"

It was Maya's voice roaring again, contaminated with that of the demons.

I still had some oxygen, reaching my brain; I still had some faculty left, which was fading away rapidly. I could still feel the knife in my right hand. The pincers of my hand were flexed to their full power.

"Yes! I am the son of a rapist and a murderer, but not a rapist and a murderer myself!"

I swung the knife and stabbed right in her heart. She screamed loudly in pain. She absolved me and started to sway back and forth with the knife in her heart. As she did so, her demonicity was fading away. Her skin was transforming back to an angelic one.

The demons inside her were howling. They began to abandon her one by one.

She fell down on her knees, her body still supported by her elbows on the ground.

She vomited blood several times. The knife had pierced her esophagus along with her heart, so that blood was being pumped in there rather than her vessels. Soon, it would be over. Her heart would not be able to stand any longer the marring that was done. Soon, there would no more blood coming out from anywhere.

She fell on her back and as she did, I saw the same Sawmya. The same beautiful damsel, who on the first sight had taken my breath away. *This time it was I, who took her breath away.*

She opened her eyes and glanced at me. I picked her head and put in my lap.

"You came Ajay? I knew you would come," she said the way she said earlier, when I found her knocked off in her home.

"I will always be there for you Sawmya. I love you and there is nobody else in my life except you."

I waited for her reply, *but there was none.*

Her eyes were still open, staring at me vacantly. I waited for them to blink, but they did not. Her pupils were fixed and dilated. I looked for the pulse, but there was none.

Her touch. It was warm, but was soon becoming colder. In a few minutes, she became extremely cold.

'*Dead are cold. Not cold, dead are extremely cold.*'

Sawmya was extremely cold. *She was dead.*

I knew it, afterall I learned it at the age of ten.

Our fugacious love story came to an end.

The dawn was about to break.

Night of the witch was over.

The Last Witch Trial had been averted.

EPILOGUE

I hope that the reason for slumping my latter name is now lucid. I was no longer imperial being called a Thakur. As I recollect the incidents that happened five years ago, the pain of the entire event re-lives itself vividly in my consciousness. Was there a rationalization for everything that happened? In the words of Mohan (the constable who accompanied us in the dark forest) *Maya had taken revenge, not only for herself, but also for all the atrocities that had been done to other women in the name of witchhood.*

However, was there the need of her to return to forbid the society against the evil custom the way she did, or could things have happened divergently?

How many more Mayas had to return from their graves to venge the barbarism that have taken place against the women in the past and are still taking place flagrantly?

Many women, even today, in some parts of our country are being tortured, raped, humiliated and murdered in the name of 'witchcraft.'

There are hundreds of them, both alive and dead, waiting for rectitude. Our courts are rancid with piles of such case files, many of which have not even seen the light of actual trial rooms.

It is simply not feasible just to list all the cases. As Professor Arya told that night in the forest, *'This night shall end soon, but there is no end to the account of the atrocities that have happened in the past in our country and the world.'*

Since then, I decided not just to sit like a common man who everyday reads about such incidents, sips up his cup of tea, grumbles to himself or his neighbor criticizing the failure of the government to stop such crimes.

I started a charity organization, which helps such women who have been at the receiving end of such false allegations. My uncle's mansion became a hospice for them. I completed my degree of Arts and later studied law. I am currently practicing as a lawyer, jousting for the victims actively rather than criticizing the failure of the government and *certainly not grumbling to myself or my neighbor.*

Gladly, Professor Arya survived the mighty blow that night, though he took around four months to recover. I got a message from him just few days ago. He has been beckoned to solve the haunting in a state parliament building. He japed in the message that already our parliaments are haunted by evil spirits wearing khadi; there was no need for another one!

Anjana though hurt that night; survived and recovered as well in the days to come. The doctors said that she was not stabbed deeply; it was just a superficial wound.

I had made it lucent to her that I shall never marry, as I could not get over with the guilt of killing Sawmya. I told her that Sawmya would always remain in my heart and so would, the repentance too. I counseled Anjana to return to Canada and get married with Ranveer, as I could never give her the place Sawmya had bedeviled in my heart. She did so. She returned to Canada. Two years later, I came to learn that she was still staying alone over there.

She had never contacted Ranveer.

She had rejected other proposals as well.

I immediately went to Canada and asked her what she was doing alone, as she did not even have any relatives there.

She replied that she did not want to come back to India and convince me to marry her. She always loved me truly and shall continue to do so forever, whether I accept her or not.

The guilt of putting knife to Sawmya's heart that night was sufficing and I could not carry further with another remorse of putting one to Anjana's heart.

I proposed to her during the visit. As time passed by, I was astonished to find that I had fallen for Anjana once again! We got married two and a half years ago, and have twin daughters who are now a year old.

There was no brawl between me and Anjana over naming the girls. The two names that notably mutated my life and conferred a design to my unworthy existence in this world; *Sawmya and Maya!*

9 789386 009296